WONDER STRUCK II

Bob McDonald
& Eric Grace

Stoddart

Published in 1991 by
Stoddart Publishing Co. Limited
34 Lesmill Road
Toronto, Canada
M3B 2T6

First published in 1989 by CBC Enterprises/
Les Enterprises Radio-Canada

CBC logo used by permission

Canadian Cataloguing in Publication Data

McDonald, Bob, 1951-
Wonderstruck II

ISBN 0-7737-5478-4

1. Science - Experiments - Juvenile literature.
I. Grace, Eric, 1948-   . II. Pearson, Gary.
III. Hemsworth, Sandra. IV. Title.

Q164.M223 1992   j502'.8   C91-095430-5

Front cover: Bob McDonald, using a slide projector, demonstrates
how fibre optics work. For a fuller explanation, see pages 55-56.

Back cover: A taste comparison shows the importance
of the nose for tasting. (See page 32.)
Experimenters (left to right): Ryan Pierce, Tammy Lee, and Lisa Daley.

*Special thanks to Liz Fox, Executive Producer of "Wonderstruck,"
for her assistance in the development of this project and to
Lesley Williams for doing the research.*

Editor: Carl Heimrich
Designer: Michael Solomon
Typesetter: Q Composition Inc.
Project Management: Sultan Street Publishing Services

Printed and bound in Canada

Table of Contents

Introduction

When *Wonderstruck* first went on the air, many people asked if there was a book of Kitchen Demos that could be done at home. After the first book was published, people asked, "Are there any more?" So here it is – another book of questions for you to ponder, and more science for you to do.

As in the first book, these are your questions, selected from the hundreds of letters written by viewers of the television program *Wonderstruck*. Thank you for doing the hardest part of the book – thinking up good questions.

Anyone who asks a good question and then tries to find the answer by observation and experiment is doing science. A scientist sees science everywhere, even in the kitchen. The demos in this book are just a few of the many possible experiments that can be done using the equipment in your kitchen cupboards. When you have done all these experiments, look carefully at the plastic bottles, soup cans, and other science apparatus in your home. With a scientific eye, you will probably discover lots of other demos that aren't in any book! Have fun!

Bob McDonald

E. Grace

What is the best way to get ketchup out of the bottle

The problem with ketchup is that it sometimes acts like a thick custard and sometimes like a flowing liquid. When the bottle has been standing for a while, the ketchup gets thick. If you try to get it out of the bottle in this state, the ketchup will either not come out at all or it will suddenly fall out in a thick glob. To make the ketchup more liquid, give the bottle a good shaking. The ketchup should then pour out of the bottle quite freely.

The reason why ketchup has this split personality is thought to be due to the shape of its molecules. They are in the form of long chains. When the ketchup is left standing, the molecules are coiled together like a pile of spaghetti. They will not flow easily like this.

When the ketchup is shaken, the molecules break apart and become looser, like the molecules in a typical liquid. This characteristic of changing from a jelly-like substance to a liquid and back again is called **thixotropy** (pronounced thick-saw-tro-pea).

Several other household substances are thixotropic. For example, margarine is quite solid when sitting in its plastic tub in the fridge, but as soon as you drag a knife across it, the margarine becomes soft and can be spread easily. Yogurt also turns from a semi-solid to a liquid after you give it a good stir. In non-drip paint, this characteristic is important. The paint flows freely under the pressure of the brush or roller, but is too thick to drip or run when left on the wall.

Through Thick and Thin

You can make your own thixotropic mixture and show its amazing characteristics to your friends.

Things you need
- 1 cup cold water
- 1½ cups cornstarch
- shallow soup dish
- wooden spoon

What to do
1. Pour the water into the dish.
2. Add the cornstarch a bit at a time, stirring to make sure it is dissolved before adding more.
3. As the mixture thickens, test it by slapping the surface with the back of the spoon. A liquid will splatter, but a thixotropic mixture does not. When all the cornstarch is dissolved, the mixture will look like thick cream.
4. Demonstrate the strange properties of the mixture to your friends. Tell them it is a dish of cream, and move the dish around a bit. The mixture will appear to be an ordinary liquid. Have your friends stand close by, then drop a baseball or similar object onto the surface of the "liquid." They will jump back, expecting to be splashed, but the mixture will now act like a jelly. If you are brave, plunge your fist down onto the mixture. It will thicken as soon as you touch it. Dabble in it with your fingers. You can scoop together a ball of the stuff, but as soon as you lift it up, it will flow off your hands.

NOTE: When you have finished with your mixture, do not pour it down the sink, or it will clog the pipes. Pour it into a container with a lid or into a plastic bag that you can tie closed, and throw it into the garbage.

Explanation
The mixture of cornstarch and water changes from liquid to solid and back again, depending on how much pressure is put on it. As a liquid, its molecules move around freely. Under pressure, its molecules have fairly fixed positions and cannot freely move. The mixture then acts more like a solid.

■ Drilling mud is a thixotropic mixture of clay and water used in oil drilling. It is pumped down a drill hole to lubricate and cool the turning end of the drill. Around the drill, where it is stirred up, the mud remains liquid. Against the sides of the drill hole, the mud forms a thick cake. This prevents the hole from collapsing, and keeps water in the soil from leaking into the hole.

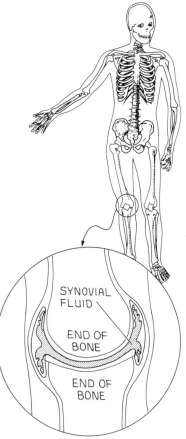

SYNOVIAL FLUID

END OF BONE

END OF BONE

■ You have a thixotropic fluid in your body. It is found in the joints, such as your elbows and knees, where two bones move against one another. The fluid flows easily during normal movements, and helps to lubricate the joint. If the joint is sharply twisted or hit, the fluid instantly becomes thicker. This helps to cushion and protect the joint against damage.

■ Quicksand is not a special sand but a thixotropic mixture of sand and water in the right combination. The sand particles are so loosely packed together that the solid-looking surface collapses when a person or animal steps on it. The mixture then becomes liquid, and the unfortunate victim sinks more deeply into it.

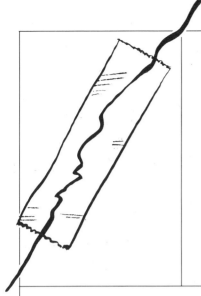

Why does sticky tape stick

It is difficult to say exactly what it is that makes one material stick to another. Part of the answer is that the molecules in the materials are attracted to one another. But attraction between molecules is what holds everything on Earth together. Why then doesn't everything stick to everything else that it touches? Obviously there's more involved, or we would soon all be in a sticky mess!

In order for two surfaces to stick together, they must be very, very close – so close that a large atom couldn't squeeze between them. Although a surface such as the cover of this book appears very smooth, if it were put under a powerful microscope, it would look like the Rocky Mountains. If you want to glue two book covers together, you must first fill in all the microscopic spaces on their surfaces. For this reason, most glues are liquid to start with. That allows the glue to flow into all the spaces on the two surfaces that are being joined.

The ability of a liquid glue to spread out depends on its surface tension – the attraction between the molecules on the surface of the liquid. If the surface tension is high, the liquid will stand in droplets, like water on a greasy plate. A good glue has a low surface tension. This lets it spread out quickly and easily to thoroughly wet all the parts being stuck together. If there are bits of dirt and dust around, they will also stop the glue getting to all parts of the surface. That's why it is important to clean the parts being glued together.

The earliest glues used by people were made from natural substances, such as tar, tree resins, honey, and egg white. The Egyptians used a paste made of flour and water over 4000 years ago. For hundreds of years, glue has been made from fish and animal bones and skin, boiled up to a sticky mess. The stickiness comes from the substance gelatin, which is also used to make jelly set. This type of glue is used in gluing furniture, binding books, and making sticky tape. Animal glues have now largely been replaced by modern synthetic glues.

Modern glues are made by mixing various chemicals, and are extremely strong. There are two general types. One type hardens after the liquid part of it has evaporated away and the glue dries out. These glues can be softened by heat or dissolved by a liquid. Common white household glue is like this. The other type hardens as a result of a chemical change that cannot be reversed. These glues cannot easily be melted or dissolved. An example is epoxy glue.

KITCHEN DEMO

Sticky Water

Can water act as a glue? Find out in this experiment.

Things you need
- flat tray or pan
- smooth plastic or metal counter or tabletop
- water

What to do
1. Pour a small puddle of water onto the smooth countertop.
2. Set the flat tray into the puddle, making sure there is no air trapped underneath.
3. Pull straight up on the tray. What happens?

Explanation
You will find it difficult to lift the tray straight off the counter because of the adhesive force of the water. (See "Did You Know?" section for more details about adhesion.)

■ What we call stickiness consists of two different forces of attraction. The attraction between two different substances is called **adhesion**. For example, on the beach, water adheres to each grain of sand. The force that attracts molecules of the same substance to one another is called **cohesion**. Molecules of water cohere to one another. The combination of adhesion and cohesion allows you to build sand castles. Dry sand will not stick together. The addition of water glues it into thick cakes.

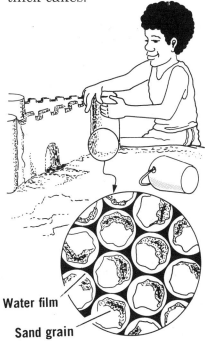

Water film

Sand grain

■ The opposite of stickiness is found in non-stick surfaces, such as you find on some frying pans. These non-stick materials have an extremely high surface tension. Fats, oils, and other liquids will not spread out and stick to them.

■ The search for better glues was prompted in the early part of this century by the need for stronger and more reliable glues to hold aircraft together. That's right! Early aircraft were made of wood. Screws and nails popped out with the vibration and stress during flight. Glues were much safer. Modern glues are so strong that they are even replacing the rivets in metal aircraft.

■ Flour and water make a good paste. With eggs and salt added, they make good pasta, such as macaroni and spaghetti. Our words "paste" and "pastry" both come from the Italian word "pasta."

■ In rare cases, things can be stuck together just by pushing them firmly together. For example, the mineral called mica is made up of very thin sheets that can be easily split apart. If freshly separated layers of mica are quickly pushed back together, they will stay together.

■ Many modern glues, such as epoxy, are made up of giant molecules called **polymers**. Polymers are built up like a construction toy, with a basic molecular unit repeated over and over.

Try this

Make a flour and water paste by adding a cup of cold water to a quarter cup of flour, stirring all the time until there are no lumps left in the mixture. Pour the paste into a large bowl. Tear up two or three sheets of newspaper into small strips, about 1 cm ($1/_2$ in) wide, and soak the strips in the paste for about fifteen minutes. Gather up the pulp into your hand and squeeze out the excess paste until you have a dough-like ball. This material is called **papier-mâché**. You can shape it like clay to make models, then leave it to dry and harden. You can then smooth it with sandpaper and paint your model.

■ Surgeons use a special glue, similar to "crazy glue," to join skin and other tissues together without using stitches or clamps.

Why are sweet things bad for your teeth?

The sugar in food doesn't rot your teeth. Neither do the millions of microscopic bacteria that live in your mouth. It is the combination of sugar and bacteria that does the harm. The bacteria feed on tiny particles of food left around your teeth and gums. After their meal, the bacteria produce acid wastes. The acid attacks the protective **enamel** on the outside of your teeth and produces cavities.

After acid has worn a hole in the enamel, other kinds of bacteria work deeper into the tooth. When the hole gets through the enamel layer into the softer material beneath (called **dentine**) you may begin to feel some sensitivity in the tooth. Although the hole in the enamel usually remains small, the rot in the dentine layer spreads out. When rot works its way deeper towards the **pulp** (**nerve**), watch out! That's when the toothache begins.

Some of the bacteria in your mouth produce a sticky material that allows them to hold onto the tooth surface. The combination of sticky material, bacteria, and food particles forms a slimy coating called **plaque** (pronounced "plak") on the surface of your teeth. If you didn't have this plaque, you would not get cavities.

To stop the plaque attack and prevent tooth decay, you need to brush and floss your teeth regularly after meals. This removes the particles of food and some of the bacteria, and prevents the buildup of plaque. Teeth should be brushed at least once every day, because the bacteria reproduce very rapidly. They can rebuild their populations within twenty-four hours, so you need daily cleaning to help keep their numbers down. Also, if plaque is not removed, it hardens and becomes a substance called **calculus** (**tartar**), which is more difficult to remove.

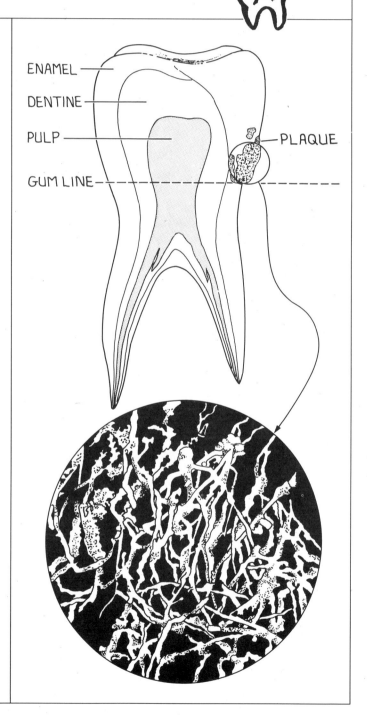

ENAMEL

DENTINE

PULP

GUM LINE

PLAQUE

KITCHEN DEMO

The Disappearing Tooth

The substance that makes enamel hard is called **calcium**. Calcium is also found in bones and eggshells. You can see for yourself the effect of acid on calcium in the following experiment.

Things you need
- an old baby tooth, a wishbone from a chicken, or a piece of eggshell
- glass jar
- vinegar

What to do
1. Put some household vinegar into a glass jar.
2. Add the tooth, bone, or shell to the vinegar and leave it standing for a few days.
3. After a few days, there will be no eggshell left at all! A tooth will take longer to disappear. A chicken wishbone will become rubbery after about a week.

Explanation
Vinegar contains acetic acid, which dissolves the calcium. Eggshells and teeth are made mostly of calcium, and they will eventually disappear if left in vinegar. When calcium is dissolved from the chicken bone, all that is left is a substance called **collagen**. This is similar to the gelatin found in jelly, which is why the bone acts like rubber. There is acid in all sorts of common household liquids. For example, try leaving a piece of eggshell in your cola drink or in apple cider.

DID YOU KNOW ???

■ Some starchy foods, especially corn chips, produce more acid plaque than sugary snacks. Peanuts and popcorn don't produce much acid plaque, but raisins do, because they are both acidic and sticky.

■ There are at least eighty different kinds of bacteria in your mouth, but only about four kinds cause decay. Different types of bacteria specialize in different parts of the mouth. Some cause decay on the sides of the teeth, some work at the gum line, and others are found only on the biting surfaces.

■ Old cheddar, Swiss, Edam, Gouda, mozzarella, Monterey Jack, and some other cheeses help fight tooth decay. Recent studies showed that when volunteers took a sugary mouth rinse after eating cheese they had no increase in plaque acidity. Volunteers who took the mouth rinse without eating cheese had a thousand-fold increase in plaque acidity. It is not known why cheese has this effect.

■ Just as acid plaque eats away teeth, so acid rain eats away statues and buildings. Many building materials, such as marble and limestone, contain calcium. Acid rain, which is often stronger than vinegar, dissolves them. In areas with a lot of acid rain, buildings, statues, and even gravestones, have suffered as much wearing away in the last twenty years as they would normally get in a thousand years. Metal structures such as bridges and cars are also eaten away by acid rain. (For more information on metal corrosion, see the question on rust on page 21.)

Try this

You can make an acid indicator from beets or red cabbage. Pour half a glass of cold water into a pan, add three or four slices of beet (or quarter of a red cabbage), and boil for five minutes. When the red liquid has cooled, pour a little of it into a jar for testing. Grape juice can also be used as an acid indicator.

   Add an alkaline substance, such as ammonia or baking soda, to the red juice. The liquid will turn yellow-green or brown. Now add something acid, such as vinegar or lemon juice. The red colour will re-appear. Take another sample of your indicator and use it to test your local rainwater. Is the rainwater more acid or less acid than vinegar?

■ Smoking is not only bad for the lungs – it's also bad for the teeth. Smoke stains leave rough surfaces on the teeth that bacteria can stick to more easily.

■ Scientists are working to develop a substance that is similar to plaque but that dissolves in water. The substance will bind to the bacteria in the mouth and prevent them from making their own sticky plaque. The artificial plaque can then be easily rinsed out of the mouth, carrying food particles and harmful bacteria with it.

■ Chewing gum may be good for you. Chewing stimulates the mouth to produce a lot of saliva, and the saliva helps neutralize the tooth-decaying acids. As with brushing, timing is important. Gum chewing should begin within five minutes of a meal, and last for at least fifteen minutes.

■ Using a toothpick is a very old human habit, according to recent research on Stone Age human teeth. The half-a-million-year-old teeth showed no sign of decay, but did have smooth, polished, semicircular grooves on their edges. Some scientists think this is evidence that human ancestors used toothpicks to remove trapped bits of food, and that the activity became a lifelong habit.

■ Dentists in the future may use laser beams to treat cavities. A laser developed by researchers in the United States vaporizes the soft tissue in dental cavities but leaves healthy enamel unharmed. The surgery will be painless. Each pulse of the laser lasts only thirty trillionths of a second – a tiny fraction of the time needed before a pain nerve will be triggered.

How did people tell the time before there were clocks ?

The oldest clock on Earth is the Earth itself. The amount of time from one sunrise to the next measures how long it takes our planet to rotate once on its axis. Ancient people probably measured time by these regular changes between daylight and darkness. Other natural events, such as sprouting leaves, heavy rains, and the migration of animals, marked the regular passing of the seasons.

All methods of measuring time, even today, depend on counting something that moves at a regular rate. The oldest type of clock made by people is the sundial, or shadow clock. It tracks the movement of the Sun across the sky by the changing position of a shadow on a dial. Unfortunately, this isn't much help at night – or on rainy days!

The next development in timekeeping was the water clock, which measured the rate at which water dripped from a cylinder. Regular marks along the inside of the cylinder allowed someone to tell the time by counting the number of lines that were uncovered. A variation on this idea is the sandglass. Like the egg-timers still used today, this measured the fixed period of time it took for sand to run from one glass container to another through a narrow passage. The largest sandglasses could measure up to an hour.

The problem with all these early clocks is that they only ran for a short period of time. As people's lives became more organized, they needed a clock that could run day and night. In addition, they needed a way of having everyone agree on what time it was, so they could all turn up for prayers or start and stop work at the same time. That is why the first mechanical clocks were put into towers. In that way, everyone in town could see them. Or, rather, everyone could hear them. Since few people could read, the earliest tower clocks had no face or hands, but simply rang a bell on the hour.

The first long-running clocks were powered by a pendulum – that is, a weight at the end of a cord or rod that swings back and forth at a fixed rate. The time it takes to make a complete swing of a pendulum depends on the length of the cord. (Test this yourself with a bit of string and a weight.) For measuring seconds, the cord needs to be about 990 mm (39 in) long. This meant that the pendulum clocks needed to be quite tall – hence the design of the "grandfather clocks," which first appeared in 1670.

Clocks powered by heavy weights were followed by spring-powered clocks and, in this century, by electric-powered clocks. Not only did clocks become more accurate and reliable, they could measure smaller and smaller amounts of time. If the regular swings of a long pendulum are needed to count the seconds, how can we measure fractions of a second?

One answer is a tuning fork – a narrow piece of metal with two prongs. If you strike a tuning fork, the prongs vibrate at a particular high frequency – say, 440 times per second. That gives a way of dividing a second into 440 parts. The tiny, rapid movements of a battery-driven tuning fork are used in some watches to move the clock mechanism.

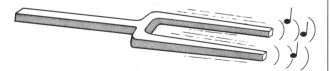

Some crystals, such as quartz, have a natural rate of vibration when electricity is passed through them. They vibrate thousands of times per second. These vibrations are so constant that a quartz crystal clock may have an error of only one second every ten years.

The ultimate in timekeeping today is the atomic clock. It is based on the natural rate of electrical and magnetic vibrations of individual atoms. These vibration rates are identical for all atoms of the same element, and are not affected by conditions around them. You can shake, drop, or rattle these atoms, and they will keep on vibrating at the same rate! Clocks based on measurements of atomic vibrations are accurate to within one second every thousand years.

A Water Clock

Making a water clock is not as easy as it might sound. How can you get your clock to drip at a regular, steady rate over a long period of time? Will the water come out of your container more slowly as time passes and there is less water in it? When you have built this water clock, you can check its accuracy against your watch or clock.

Things you need
- clean, empty, plastic dishwashing-liquid bottle
- string about 20 cm (8 in) long
- clear glass or plastic jar
- ruler
- marker (or grease pencil, china marker)

What to do
1. Make a hole in the bottom of the plastic bottle.

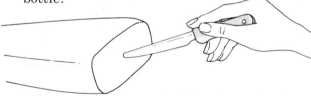

2. Tie a knot at one end of the piece of string and pull the string through the hole so the knot is inside the bottle.

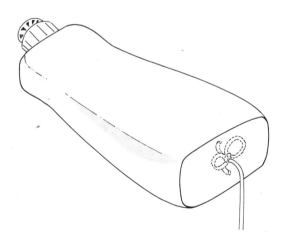

3. Fill the plastic bottle with water, screw the top tight, then carefully lay the bottle on its side at the edge of a shelf or table, with the string hanging down.
4. Place the empty jar directly below the end of the string to catch the drips.

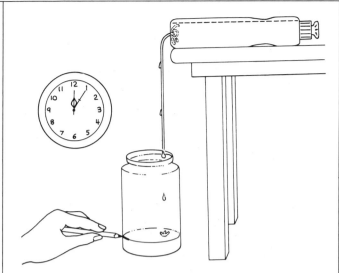

5. After five minutes, mark the water level on the side of the jar.
6. Measure the height to your mark, then draw five more lines, all the same distance apart, on the side of the jar.

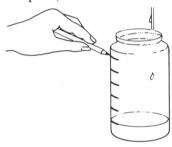

7. Every five minutes, check if the water level is at one of the marks.

RIGHT ON TIME!

Does your water clock speed up or slow down? If so, how could you make it more accurate?

Explanation
The accuracy of the water clock depends on getting a regular rate of drips. If the bottle was upright, water pressure would make the water come out fast at first and then slow down as the water level in the bottle fell. The string draws the water out of the bottle at a constant rate.

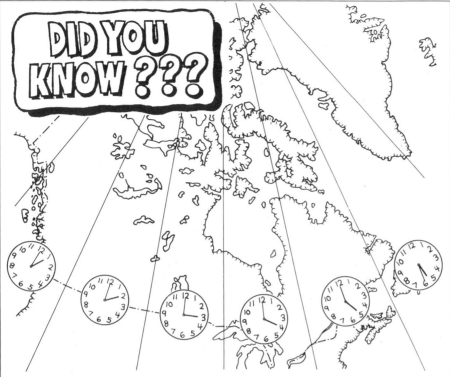

DID YOU KNOW ???

■ During the last century, many towns kept their own system of time. If you travelled from one province to the next, you might have had to change your watch ten times or more. As travel by train grew popular, and more people moved quickly from place to place, the many different systems of time became confusing. A Canadian, Sir Sanford Fleming, suggested a system of standard time that would allow people to know what the time was in other places, not only in different parts of Canada but all around the world. Because there are twenty-four hours in a day, he proposed dividing the world into twenty-four time zones. Within each zone, all clocks would show the same time. In the next zone to the west, clocks would be one hour behind, while in the zone to the east, they would show one hour ahead. Fleming's system was accepted at an international conference held in 1884 in Washington, D.C.

■ Physicist Albert Einstein astonished everyone by claiming that time itself is not steady, but it can speed up or slow down. Time, he said, is relative. Einstein predicted that time would slow down at high speeds, or high gravity. His prediction was proved by an experiment using atomic clocks. A clock flown around the Earth at high speed on a jet was found to run slower than an identical clock left behind on the ground.

■ Some animals have a built-in "biological clock" that tells them when to do certain things. A fiddler crab, for example, moves up and down the beach according to the rhythms of the Moon and the Sun. If a crab from the Atlantic coast in eastern Canada is suddenly flown to the Pacific coast in the west, it will continue to move up and down the beach of its new home according to the time on the east coast – even though the Sun rises and sets about three hours later in the west. The crab is moving to its internal clock. People have a similar experience when they suffer from "jet lag." They may arrive in Europe at breakfast time, but they feel as if it is the middle of the night.

■ Wristwatches did not become popular until the beginning of this century. Before then, most watches were attached to a chain and were carried around in a pocket. A Swiss wristwatch exhibited in 1914 was considered to be just a passing fad. Today, about eighty million wristwatches are made worldwide every year!

20

Why do some metals rust and others don't

Rust forms only on metals that contain iron. It is the result of a chemical reaction between the iron and the moisture and oxygen in the air. Rust can be prevented by keeping oxygen and moisture from the surface of the iron-containing metal.

In nature, few metals are found in a pure form. Iron, for example, is mined as iron ore – a mixture of iron compounds. Pure iron is extracted from the ore by melting and purifying it. Rusting reverses this process, turning the pure iron back into an iron compound. Rust can be thought of as a more natural and chemically stable form of iron. No wonder the battle to prevent rust forming on cars, bridges, and buildings is never-ending!

The process of rusting actually takes place in two steps. First, the iron is dissolved. It is dissolved by a weak acid that is formed when water sitting on the metal combines with carbon dioxide gas from the air. The acid dissolves the iron. Acid rain, or salt from sea spray or road salt, speeds up this part of the process. In the second step, the dissolved iron reacts with oxygen to form **iron oxide** – the soft, brown-red coating that we call rust.

A common way of protecting iron and steel (a harder form of iron that contains carbon) is to cover it with a thin layer of another material, such as paint or plastic. This protects the metal from contact with moisture and air. Unfortunately, if the protective layer is scratched, the metal underneath is exposed and rusting can start.

Another method of protection, used on metal items such as garbage cans, pails, fencing, and nails, is called **galvanizing**. This coats the iron-containing metal with a lighter metal called **zinc**. The zinc reacts even more readily with oxygen to form a fine white powder. If there is a scratch in the galvanized metal, the zinc will corrode first before the iron does.

DON'T WORRY ABOUT RUSTING... IT IS PERFECTLY NATURAL!

KITCHEN DEMO

Rust Sucks

Things you need
- new, clean steel wool
- vinegar
- glass bottle with small opening
- pencil
- balloon

What to do
1. Soak a piece of steel wool in vinegar for about five minutes.
2. Carefully pull the steel wool apart and poke the metal threads into a bottle, using a pencil.

3. Add a few drops of water to the bottle.

4. Stretch the lip of a balloon over the mouth of the bottle, then stand the bottle in a warm place.

5. Watch what happens to the balloon over the next twenty-four hours.

Explanation
The acidic vinegar removes the protective surface from the steel wool. In the warm, damp air inside the bottle, the steel quickly starts to rust. The formation of the red iron oxide (rust) uses up oxygen from the air, and this reduces the air pressure inside the bottle. The air pressure outside then pushes the balloon into the bottle.

MARS IS NICE BUT EARTH ISN'T AS RUSTED!

■ Naturally-occurring iron oxide pigments give the rocks and soil in some parts of the world a reddish rust colour. Early in human history these rocks were ground up and used as dyes to colour paints and fabrics.

■ The entire Earth is rusting! The surface of the Earth contains many different metals which react with oxygen from the air to form metal oxides. Most of the Earth's common rocks are oxides. It is fortunate that green plants continually produce oxygen, because rocks alone would otherwise use up all the atmosphere's oxygen in only a few hundred years!

■ The red colour of Mars is due to the oxidation of its surface rocks. There is little oxygen in the Martian atmosphere because it was all used up in the rocks.

■ An iron oxide similar to rust is used to make a brightly-coloured pigment called Venetian red. When powdered, this is called "jeweller's rouge" and is used for polishing precious metals and diamonds.

■ Take a look at the tape in your cassettes. Its rusty red-brown colour is a form of iron oxide. The tiny particles of iron oxide powder are coated onto a thin strip of plastic. During a recording, electrical signals from the sound create magnetic fields at the recording head. The magnetism changes the positions of the iron particles. The tape is therefore imprinted with a magnetic record of the electrical signal.

Try this

Make your own magic ink from rust. Put a piece of clean steel wool in a jar and cover it with white vinegar. Set the jar in a pan of hot water. Meanwhile, put four tea bags into a cup and cover them with boiling water.

When both solutions are cool, mix them in equal amounts and stir. Dip a finger or brush in the mixture and write on a sheet of paper. Although you won't see anything at first, your writing will gradually turn black. That is because the chemical made by the mixture of vinegar, steel, and tea is altered by exposure to the air. It forms another chemical that is black.

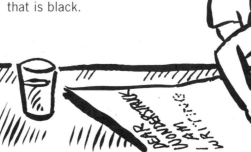

How can some people lie down on a bed of nails

The secret of this trick is to have enough nails! If you lie on only one nail, your entire weight pushes down on a single point. The amount of pressure on the point of the nail is more than enough to drive the nail into your flesh. Now imagine lying down on two nails. The force of your weight on each nail is halved. (It's still enough to drive the nails in, however!). If you lie on one hundred nails, the pressure on each point will be only one one-hundredth of your weight. On two hundred nails, it will be one two-hundredths of your weight, and so on. At a certain number of nails, the pressure is distributed over so many nails that there is not enough force on any particular point to be able to drive it into your flesh.

Pressure is the amount of force per unit of area. It is possible for a fairly small mass to exert a surprisingly large amount of pressure, if it is all concentrated in a small area. For example, consider the pressure you exert when you stand on the floor. It is easy to calculate, as this example shows:

Your weight = 50 kg
The area of the bottom of your shoes = 150 cm²
The pressure you exert on the floor = 50/150 = 0.33 kg/cm²

Now, imagine you have changed into a pair of ice skates. The area of the ice skates that touches the ice is only 10 cm². What is the pressure you exert on the ice? Calculate it as follows:

Your weight = 50 kg
The area of the bottom of your skates = 10 cm²
The pressure you exert on the ice = 50/10 = 5 kg/cm²

You can see from these calculations that you exert fifteen times more pressure when wearing your skates than you do when wearing shoes. You haven't got fifteen times heavier, you are just putting all your weight on a smaller area. In the metric system of measurement, pressure is expressed in units called pascals.

A 50 kg woman standing on one stiletto heel exerts 5 times more pressure than a 9000 kg elephant standing on one leg.

KITCHEN DEMO

Putting on the Pressure

This experiment shows the difference between pressure and mass.

Things you need
- clay or Plasticine
- 1-L bottle of pop

What to do

1. Roll the clay into a ball and then flatten it until you have a thick disc about the size of your palm.

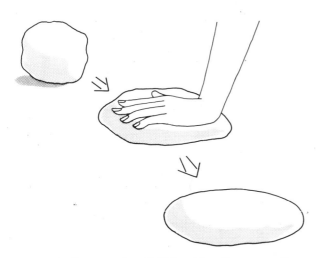

2. Carefully stand a full bottle of pop on the clay.

3. Remove the bottle and observe the depression that it made in the disc of clay.

4. Turn the bottle over and carefully stand it on its cap in the centre of the clay disc. Gently help the bottle to stay balanced if necessary, but do not push down on it.

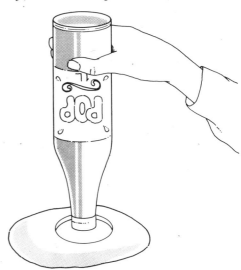

5. Remove the bottle and look at the depression it left in the clay. Compare the depth of the mark made by the top of the bottle with the depression made by the bottom of the bottle. How can you explain the difference?

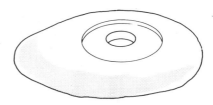

Explanation

The mass of the bottle was concentrated in a smaller area when the bottle was standing on its top. It therefore exerted a greater pressure and made a deeper mark.

DID YOU KNOW ???

■ A camel is able to travel easily over the soft desert sands without sinking in because it has very broad feet. These distribute its mass over a large area, and therefore exert less pressure on the sand than smaller feet would. Snowshoes do the same thing, only on snow.

■ It is not only solid things that exert pressure. Gases and liquids do so as well. The weight of the atmosphere pushing down on the Earth's surface is equal to a pressure of about 1 kg/cm^2 at sea level. Air pressure gets less if you climb up a mountain or fly in a plane, because there is less atmosphere above you. That is why the cabin of an airline must be pressurized during a flight.

■ Water is stronger than rock. Small drops of rain beating against a rock exert enough pressure to wear the rock away after many years. In mining, jets of water are used as drills. Forced from a nozzle at a pressure of hundreds of kilograms per square centimetre, the stream of water blasts away chunks of rock.

■ Artificial diamonds can be made by putting carbon under pressure. Before you rush out and stand on some carbon, however, you should know that it takes a pressure of 55 000 kg/cm^2 – and a temperature of about 1500°C. Even then, the diamonds produced are only of industrial quality – not suitable for a ring or brooch.

■ To save a person who has fallen through thin ice, rescuers lie down flat on the ice in order to reach the person. By spreading their body mass over a large area, they do not exert enough pressure on the ice to break it.

■ Snow under pressure becomes ice. That is how glaciers are formed. On mountain tops and at the poles, snow piles up in deep layers that do not melt from year to year. The weight of all that snow turns the bottom of the snow heaps into ice.

■ The next time you are in a bank, look at the spots on the floor where customers stand in front of the tellers. These areas usually have distinctive pitting, made by years of pressure from people standing in high heels.

■ Cars with wide, racing-type tires become stuck in snow more easily than cars with standard tires. The car with narrower tires exerts more pressure on the snow and so gets better traction.

Why are there always coconut trees on tropical islands

As postcards and cartoons show, coconut trees grow on islands and along tropical coasts near gently sloping beaches – and that is a clue to the answer. Inside the coconuts are the seeds of this tree. Unlike most plant seeds, coconuts can float and survive for many weeks in sea water. Washed from their beaches by the waves, coconuts are carried across the sea from island to island and from shore to shore. It is thought that coconut trees once grew only in India and Malaya. Riding the ocean currents, they have now spread to tropical coasts around the world.

Coconuts are just one example of the ways plants have found to move around. Because plants cannot walk, run, fly, or swim like animals, they depend on their seeds to spread themselves from place to place. If plants just dropped their seeds around them, they would soon run out of space to grow. Each new plant would have to compete with its parent for sunlight and water. By finding a way to move their seeds around, there is a chance that some of the plant's seeds will settle in a new area that is suitable for them to grow.

Many seeds – the jet-setters of the plant world – travel by air. Some, like dandelions, are carried by light, fluffy parachutes that can catch the lightest breeze. Larger seeds, such as those of the maple tree, have developed wings that slow their fall to the ground and allow them to be twirled away on a passing wind.

In forests, where dense growth keeps out the wind, many trees depend on animals to transport their seeds. The seeds may have hooks, bristles, or sticky coats that catch on passing fur or feathers. The familiar burr that grabs your sweater or mitts is like this. Other forest trees wrap their seeds inside a tasty fruit. They are then carried off inside a bird or mammal when the animal eats the fruit. The seed passes through the animal without being digested and is later deposited on the ground with the animal's droppings.

Not all plants wait around for wind or animals to carry their seeds. Some take an active role and fire their seeds from them like little missiles. This is done, for example, by some seed pods that grow tight as they dry out. Eventually, the tight pod bursts open, shooting out the seeds.

Few plants travel by water. Some streamside species such as water lilies send off their seeds in small floating packages, while the seeds of marsh and bog plants are often carried away in the mud sticking to the feet of wading birds. The coconut is truly an adventurer among plants. Its reward for braving the open seas is to be the dominant tree on many a far-flung island.

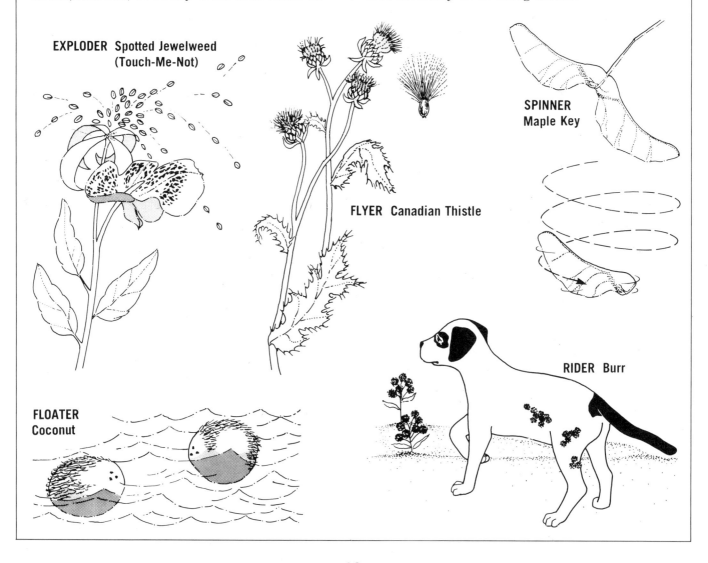

EXPLODER Spotted Jewelweed (Touch-Me-Not)

FLYER Canadian Thistle

SPINNER Maple Key

RIDER Burr

FLOATER Coconut

KITCHEN DEMO

Paper Seeds

The maple seed has an effective design for catching the air. Engineers have determined that it works 1.2 times as efficiently as the best designed windmill blades. You can make your own twirling seed in the following demonstration.

Things you need
- construction paper
- ruler
- pencil
- scissors
- paper clip

What to do
1. Cut two pieces of paper about 7 cm × 10 cm each.
2. Make a 7 cm cut along the centre of each piece.

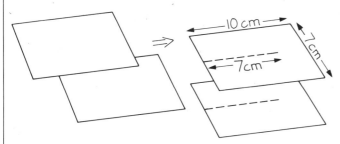

3. Hold one sheet up by the base and fold the left wing towards you and the right wing away from you.

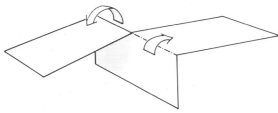

4. Hold up the second sheet and fold the right wing towards you and the left wing away from you.

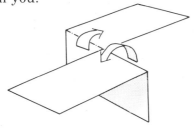

5. Fasten a small paper clip to the centre of the body of each paper seed.

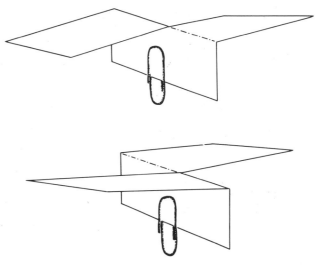

6. Hold each seed above your head and let them go.

Explanation
One seed spins clockwise and the other spins counterclockwise. The spinning movement is caused by air escaping from under the wings. Where the air runs into the body of the seed, it pushes it forward, causing the seed to turn.

■ The coconut seed is actually very tiny. The coconut that you buy in the store is mostly just the seed's packaging. The white coconut "meat" and the milk are made by the tree to provide nourishment for the seed on a long voyage.

Try this

In the late summer or fall, when many seeds are ready to be dispersed, you can collect hooked and sticky seeds with your own version of a small, furry animal. Get an old, large woolly sock and stuff it with newspapers. This is your sock animal. Tie a length of string around the opening of the sock, with enough string left to make a "leash." Take a walk through a nearby woods or field, pulling your sock animal behind you. At the end of your walk, pull off all the burrs and other hooked seeds that are clinging to the sock. See if you can get the seeds to grow to find out what plants they're from.

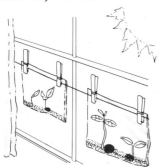

You can make a simple greenhouse for your seeds from a clear plastic bag. Just put a few drops of water in the bottom of the bag, drop in two or three seeds, and staple the top of the bag closed. You can hang several bags like this from a piece of string across the window, using clothes pins.

■ The coconut is a member of the palm tree family, which includes date trees and ornamental palms. There are 2600 known species of palm, most of them growing in the tropics.

■ The seeds of some pine trees are not released from their cone until it has been burned. This amazing feature is an adaptation to the fires that often sweep through the northern pine forests. After a fire is the best time for a new tree to start growing. There is lots of open sunny space, and the soil is enriched by the ashes of the burned trees.

■ The sticky, bullet-shaped seeds of the parasitic dwarf mistletoe are shot from the plant at an incredible speed of twenty four metres per second. They fly with explosive force for up to eighteen metres before sticking to a branch of a nearby tree. There they send roots into the tree and begin their life as a parasite.

■ A member of the geranium family that lives in deserts is called the **storksbill** because its seeds have long, pointed beaks. When the seeds are ripe, they twist into a spiral and drop to the ground. When it rains, the spiral beaks absorb water and straighten out, driving the seeds into the earth.

■ For people in the tropics, the coconut tree is like a department store. Its oil is used for making soap, shampoo, detergent, margarine, rubber, and brake fluid. The dried meat can be eaten raw or cooked, or used to feed livestock, or to make fertilizer. The stiff fibres on the outside of the coconut are made into brushes, ropes, matting, and fishing nets, while baskets are made from the leaves. Palm wine and vinegar are made from the flower buds, and the tree trunks provide timber for construction. The people of Indonesia claim that the coconut has as many uses as there are days in the year.

■ A study of the flowering plants on different islands shows that they get to the islands in different ways. On low-lying coral atolls, most of the plants arrive by drifting on the ocean. Many of the plants on mountainous islands are carried there by birds, while the wind carries seeds to many of the islands that lie close to a mainland.

■ In the late 1400s, Leonardo da Vinci designed and drew a type of helicopter based on his observation of the spinning movement of maple tree seeds. Even earlier than that, the Chinese and Europeans made helicopter toys. The whirligig was a popular medieval children's toy, but helicopters did not become a reality until this century. The first successful powered helicopter was not flown until 1940.

Why can't I taste anything when I have a cold

The flavour of food comes mostly from its smell. When you have a cold, your nose is blocked. When you can't smell your food, it tastes dull and bland.

The flavour of what you eat actually depends on many different things, including its taste, smell, temperature and texture. (If you doubt the importance of temperature and texture, compare the flavour of a hot, crisp french fry with that of a cold, limp one.) The senses of smell and taste are both based on chemicals. They should really be called our chemical senses. Your nose detects chemicals that are carried through the air. Your tongue detects chemicals that touch them. The two senses work together, but your nose is thousands of times more sensitive than your taste buds.

It used to be thought that there were four basic tastes: salt, sweet, bitter, and sour – and that all other tastes were combinations of these. It was also believed that taste buds on different parts of the tongue were sensitive to different basic tastes. Experiments on individual taste buds show that things are more complicated than this. Since each taste bud has fifty nerve fibres entering it, that's not surprising!

For complexity, however, the nose has the tongue licked. It can tell the difference between about four thousand different chemical molecules. Some individual cells inside the nose detect a huge variety of smells, while others pick out only one smell, and can detect it in very tiny amounts.

Most food smells are made up of many different chemicals. For example, the smell of fresh bread consists of 70 different chemicals, and the scent of coffee drifting through the air carries 103 separate chemicals. A strawberry smell has 35 chemicals, and our noses are sensitive enough to distinguish if a strawberry has been crushed, or if it is over-ripe.

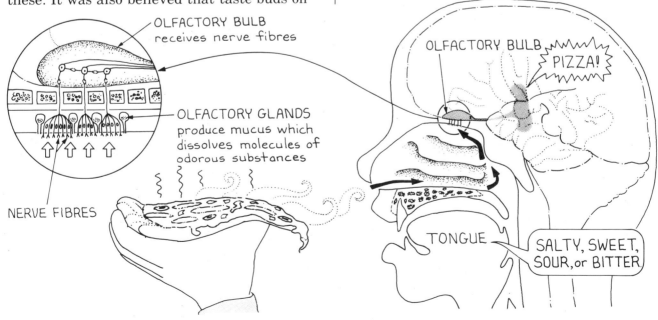

OLFACTORY BULB receives nerve fibres

OLFACTORY GLANDS produce mucus which dissolves molecules of odorous substances

NERVE FIBRES

OLFACTORY BULB

PIZZA!

TONGUE

SALTY, SWEET, SOUR, or BITTER

KITCHEN DEMO

The Nose Knows

To prove the importance of your nose for tasting, try to identify some different foods with your tongue alone.

Things you need
- samples of food with similar textures, for example:
  — raw potato, turnip, apple, and onion
  — cooked peas and baked beans
  — different flavours of jelly
  — different types of cheese (for the gourmet only!)
- handkerchief
- a friend

What to do
1. Have your friend prepare samples of the foods you are testing. Make sure each sample is about the same size and shape.
2. Tie on the handkerchief as a blindfold, hold your nose tightly, and put out your tongue.
3. Have your friend place a sample of food on your tongue. Say what you think the food is. Now bite the sample.
4. Repeat the test with each sample of food. When the test is complete, your friend will tell you how often you were correct.

Explanation
When you cannot smell food, it has little taste. The feel and texture give you some clues about the food you are eating.

DID YOU KNOW ???

■ Your sense of taste is most sensitive when the food is close to body temperature. Compare the taste of a piece of cheese straight from the fridge with a piece of the same cheese at room temperature.

■ Cells that are sensitive to unpleasant chemicals are also found in your eyes as well as your nose. That is why some strong smells make your eyes water.

■ The natural gas used in many homes for cooking and heating has no smell. Because it is important to know if gas is leaking, the gas companies add a smell to it before sending it out into homes.

■ Salmon that swim from the Pacific Ocean up west coast rivers to breed find their way by smell. The fish can detect small differences in the smell of the water from different rivers, and always return to the river in which they were born.

■ Many animals use smell to communicate. For example, the urine of a fox or a deer can tell other animals whether that individual is sick, or ready to breed, or is a dominant animal.

■ The Supersniffer is a Canadian invention that can detect small quantities of different chemicals. The small, easily-carried machine is a hundred times as sensitive as a dog's nose. It can be used, for example, at airports to sniff out drugs or explosives.

■ Smells are sometimes connected with things that have made strong impressions on us and are remembered for many years. The smell of a classroom, a particular perfume, a hospital, or new-mown hay, for example, can bring back vivid memories.

■ Our noses can detect the smell of a skunk in quantities as small as only 360 molecules – a microscopic amount.

■ Has the cat got your tongue? Maybe it wishes it had, because a cat's tongue doesn't have any chemical receptors for sugar. A dog's tongue does, however, which may be why a dog will beg for sweet treats while a cat just looks the other way.

■ Sharks can detect blood in the water in quantities of much less than one part per million.

Try this

Tongue Tricks

Hold your nose and place a few orange drink crystals on your tongue. Can you taste the orange? Now take a deep breath.

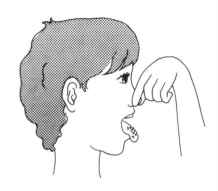

Can you put your tongue into these shapes? Can your family or friends? The ability to curl the tongue in certain ways is inherited.

Tongue Twister

Try saying this sentence quickly: The sixth sheik's sixth sheep is sick.

■ Most birds do not have a strong sense of taste. The average pigeon has only 37 taste buds, compared with 9000 in people and 17 000 in rabbits.

BIRDS HAVE NO TASTE!

■ As with the other senses, the sense of taste is learned. Some tastes, such as spinach or certain strong cheeses, are not immediately appealing. After several tries, however, the senses can adapt to their flavour. That is why gourmets may enjoy foods that others find revolting, and people from different countries and cultures like different tastes.

■ The ability to taste certain substances is inherited. For example, some people find the chemical phenylthiocarbamide tastes bitter, while others cannot taste it at all. About thirty-five per cent of Europeans are non-tasters of this chemical.

■ Pregnancy, like head colds, can disturb the sense of taste and smell. Pregnant women often find they dislike the smell of foods they once enjoyed.

■ The flickering, forked tongue of a snake or lizard is literally tasting the air. After it is waved around, the tip of the tongue is put in a special organ in the roof of the mouth. The organ detects any chemicals from the air that have stuck to the tongue. Maybe that's why people speak of their tongues hanging out when they're hungry. It could be a way to get an advance taste of the food!

■ Not all animals detect the taste of their food through their tongues. Some frogs and toads have taste-sensitive cells on their cheeks and lips, and some fish have them on their fins and tails. Flies have chemical-sensitive cells in their feet.

■ You can see that taste is a chemical sense if you look at the labels on some packages of food. The food industry has developed many artificial chemicals that have a taste and smell you can't tell from those of the real thing.

Why do some foods spoil quickly and others don't

Food rots when microscopic organisms, such as fungi and bacteria, start to live and grow on it. These organisms are found everywhere. They are in the air, on shelves and tabletops, and on your skin. When food is left exposed, or is touched by fingers, it is easy for micro-organisms to settle on it, feed, and build up their numbers. You can keep food from spoiling quickly by storing it in a sealed container. Food is also protected by freezing it or drying it or by adding chemicals to it that prevent the micro-organisms from growing.

Bacterial Culture

Although some types of micro-organisms spoil our food, we use other micro-organisms to make food. For example, if you look at the list of ingredients on a container of yogurt or sour cream, you will see that they contain "bacterial culture." The bacteria produce the yogurt and sour cream from milk. Other types of micro-organisms make cheese from milk. Yeast, which is a type of fungus, is used by bakers to make traditional bread. The yeast is added to the dough mixture, where it feeds on the sugar and produces tiny bubbles of carbon dioxide gas. This gas is what makes the bread rise and forms the tiny holes that you see in a slice of bread. Other foods that micro-organisms help produce are wine, pickles, and chocolate.

HEY GLADYS, GIVE ME A HAND WITH THIS LID.

SORRY, I DON'T HAVE HANDS!

MAYONNAISE

KITCHEN DEMO

Rising with Yeast

You can buy dried yeast in packets at the supermarket. In this experiment, you can show that yeast makes carbon dioxide gas from sugar.

Things you need
- packet of dried yeast
- 3 bottles
- 3 balloons
- sugar
- water
- sticky labels and marker

What to do
1. Measure three cups of water into a saucepan or kettle, boil it, and let it cool.
2. Pour one cup of the cooled water into each of the three bottles.

3. Add two teaspoons of sugar to two of the bottles and shake them around until the sugar is dissolved. Label the bottles with the letter "S."

4. Add one teaspoon of yeast to the third bottle and label the bottle "Y."
5. Add one teaspoon of yeast to one of the bottles containing sugar, and add "Y" to the bottle label. You should now have one bottle containing sugar and water, one with yeast and water, and one with sugar, yeast, and water.

6. Stretch the balloons a few times, and place a balloon over the mouth of each bottle.

7. Leave the bottles in a warm place for one or two days and watch what happens.

Explanation
The balloon over the bottle with the sugar and yeast will fill with carbon dioxide gas, made by the yeast feeding on the sugar. The other two bottles are used as controls. Their balloons do not fill up, proving that sugar and yeast on their own do not produce the gas.

DID YOU KNOW ???

■ Micro-organisms are so small that you cannot usually see them without a microscope. To get some idea of how small they are, imagine you are a bacterium standing on the head of a pin. The distance across the pin will seem as big to the bacterium as a length of seventy-five metres looks to you. (Seventy-five metres is three-quarters the length of a football field.)

■ Some micro-organisms cause diseases, such as pneumonia, strep throat, and smallpox. Other micro-organisms help protect us from disease. Penicillin, for example, is produced by a type of fungus. It is used by doctors to destroy many types of bacteria.

■ If there were no micro-organisms, animals and plants could not survive. Micro-organisms break down dead animals and plants, turning them into chemicals that pass back into the soil, air, and water. They are the world's greatest recyclers. Without them, dead plants and animals would simply pile up, and the cycle of life would come to a grinding halt.

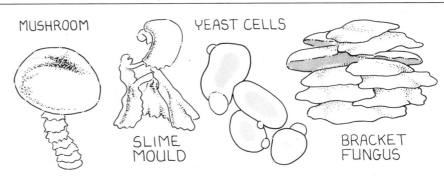

MUSHROOM   YEAST CELLS

SLIME MOULD   BRACKET FUNGUS

■ The organisms we call fungi have a wide range of appearances – from the single-celled yeast, to mildew and mould, to mushrooms and toadstools. Fungi are neither plants nor animals. They are classified by scientists in a group of their own.

■ One reason why it is risky to leave food uncovered is that micro-organisms can reproduce very rapidly. A few organisms landing on a rich supply of food can grow to a huge number in a surprisingly short time. They reproduce by splitting in two. With each split the population is doubled. Under ideal conditions, each bacterium can grow to full size and divide in only twenty minutes.

Try this

Imagine you must fill a bucket with water in the following way. First, you put in one teaspoonful of water. Next, you add two spoonfuls. The third time, you add four, then eight, and so on, doubling the amount of water you add each time. How many times must you add water to the bucket before it is full? Calculate the answer, or try the experiment, using a measuring cup when you get to large numbers (there are about fourteen teaspoons in a quarter of a cup). This experiment will give you an idea of how rapidly a population can grow when the numbers double each time.

■ All plants and animals – including you – are covered with millions of micro-organisms. In fact, there are more micro-organisms living around your mouth and gums than there are humans living on the entire planet! Don't worry, though. The vast majority of them are harmless. (See the question on teeth on page 14 for more information about the micro-organisms in your mouth.)

MORE SUGAR?

NO, I DON'T WANT TO DRY OUT.

■ Although micro-organisms like sugar, too much of it will keep them away. Crystallized fruits and candy do not spoil very easily because the strong sugar solution around them will draw the fluids out of micro-organisms and dry them out. For the same reason, some foods, such as pork, are preserved by salting.

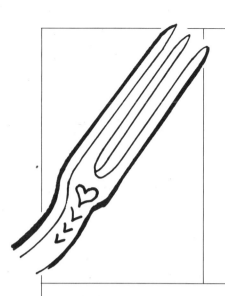

Can my senses be fooled

What we sense depends as much on our brain as on our eyes, nose, ears, fingers, and tongue. Our brain interprets the information it gets from the sense organs, using past experiences. Because of this, we can easily be fooled by the unexpected.

For example, how do you know if something is hot or cold? When you touch it, cells in your skin that are sensitive to temperature send nerve signals to your brain. One way to confuse your brain is to give it two opposite bits of sensory information at the same time, as in the following example.

Imagine you have three large bowls. Fill one with very cold water, one with hot water (not hot enough to burn your fingers!), and one with lukewarm water. Place the bowls in a row on the table, with the lukewarm water in the centre. Dip one hand in the cold water and your other hand in the hot water and leave them there for two minutes. Quickly shake the water from your hands and dip both hands at once into the centre bowl. How do they feel? The hand that's been in cold water will feel warm, while the hand that's been in hot water will feel cold. Yet they are both in the same water!

Experiments such as this show that we must learn how to interpret our sense of touch. The same is true of all the other senses. We must learn how to see, smell, taste, and hear.

KITCHEN DEMO

A. Fooling Your Eyes

Things you need
● penny

What to do
Can you put a penny on this table? After you answer, try it. Were you fooled?

Explanation
Your experience of tables tells you that they are rectangular in shape. Your brain therefore interprets what you see in the drawing as a rectangle. A rectangle with sides as long as those of the table in the drawing would easily hold a penny. In fact, however, the tabletop in the drawing is a parallelogram. Your eyes send the information to your brain, but your brain has been fooled by its own experience.

B. Fooling Your Ears

Things you need
● piece of stiff cellophane paper

Get a piece of stiff cellophane paper, such as the wrapping from a box of cookies or breakfast cereal.

What to do
Close your eyes and imagine a blazing forest fire, then lightly squeeze and crumple the paper in your hand.

Explanation
The sound of the paper is very like that of wood burning vigorously. If you imagine a fire, the sound is even more lifelike. Your senses of sight and sound often work together. It is sometimes difficult to distinguish similar sounds from one another without practice if you cannot see what is causing the sound. Another common example of this is the sound of wind rustling in the trees. This sound is very like that made by a waterfall, and you can easily imagine there is a waterfall just out of sight in the forest. On the radio, sound effects people often use one sound to represent something else. Make your own sound effects by making different sounds, closing your eyes, and thinking what else might sound like that.

■ Here's a way to discover that you really do learn how to see things, and that you can improve your ability to see. Scan several pages of a book (this one will do) and pick out every letter "e" on each page. You will find that after three or four pages you get much quicker and more accurate at doing this. Now look for the two-letter combination "ea." When you concentrate on looking for something very particular in this way, your brain holds what is called a "searching image." It ignores everything that is not like this image, and so speeds up your ability to search quickly.

■ Here's a way to improve your sense of touch. With a friend, collect about ten similar leaves. Put on a blindfold and have your friend hand you a leaf. Carefully feel all over the leaf with your fingers. Get to know every vein and outline. When you think you know it, have your friend put the leaf back with the others. Take off the blindfold and pick out your leaf from the pile. If you find this difficult at first, you will soon improve after a few tries. Change places with your friend and see how well your friend does.

■ The ability of some animals to see at night may depend on the temperature. You see things when particles of light hit the sensitive layer at the back of your eye and cause changes in the shape of molecules there. The problem is that these molecules also change their shape from time to time by normal molecular movements. When it gets warm, the movements occur more often. This could produce "visions" of things that aren't really there. Fortunately, the changes in the molecules caused by light far outnumber the changes caused by normal movements – except when there is not very much light around. Scientists have tested this idea with frogs and toads. Starting in the dark, they placed a white dummy of a worm in front of the animals. The scientists gradually increased the light until the animals snapped at the worm, showing that they could see it. They repeated the experiment at different temperatures. Sure enough, at lower temperatures, the animals could see the worm with less light.

What holds the balcony up in a cinema or theatre

The huge overhanging theatre balconies with their hundreds of seats don't seem to be supported by very much, but in fact they are examples of a common type of structure called a **cantilever**.

A cantilever is really just a beam that is supported at one end only instead of two. To understand how beams and cantilevers support large weights, get a drinking straw that has pleats in the middle and balance it across the tops of two mugs or glasses.

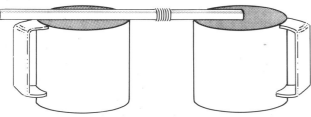

You now have a simple beam supported at two ends. Gently push down with your finger near the centre of the straw and look at what happens to the pleats. Those on the top side are squeezed together as the beam bends, while the pleats on the underside are spread apart. Engineers call these two different stresses on a beam **compression** and **tension**. Compression takes place when something is being squashed, like the top of your straw beam. Tension takes place when something is being pulled apart, like the bottom of the beam. To stop a beam from bending under a weight it needs to resist compression.

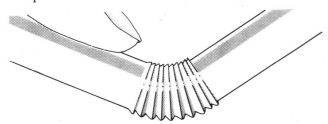

Now hold one end of the straw firmly on top of one glass and take the other glass away. Gently push down on your cantilever and watch the pleats. The bending cantilever is stressed in the opposite way to a bending beam. This time, the underside is squashed together and the top side spreads apart, or is under tension. In other words, a cantilever must have a high tensile strength to resist bending. Until about a hundred years ago, there were no suitable materials with enough tensile strength that could be used to build large cantilevers. Structural steel has this strength, however, and is now used to build cantilevers in bridges, construction cranes, and theatre balconies.

KITCHEN DEMO

Bridge of Knives

Here's a challenge to test your knowledge of construction stresses and strains.

Things you need
- 3 table knives
- 4 cups

What to do
1. Set three of the cups on a table to form a triangle with its sides slightly longer than the length of the knives.
2. Use the knives to build a bridge that will support the fourth cup.

Explanation
Although it doesn't seem so at first, each knife is being supported at both ends in this structure. The added weight of the fifth cup bends each knife down slightly and balances the stresses of compression and tension. The upward and downward forces are equal, and friction stops the knives from sliding sideways.

DID YOU KNOW ???

■ The longest cantilever bridge in the world spans the St. Lawrence River in Quebec. When it was first built, in 1904, the stresses were wrongly calculated. The bridge collapsed just when it was nearly complete, killing seventy-five people. It was redesigned and rebuilt, and the bridge was opened in 1918.

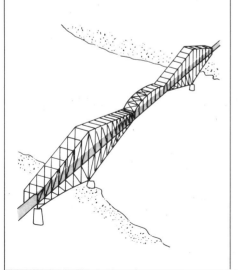

■ A lot of the strength in a structure comes from its design, rather than from the materials it is made with. For example, see how much weight you can support on a bridge made from a strip of ordinary cardboard and one made from a strip of corrugated cardboard, such as that used in grocery boxes. The folds of thin card at the centre of the corrugated cardboard form a series of triangles that add greatly to the strength. Next time you go out, look for triangles in building structures around you. You will see them in shopping malls, electricity pylons, cranes, bridges, and many other places.

Try this

With a friend, hold a wooden metrestick by the ends and hang a weight on it until the metrestick bends. Now turn the stick on edge. After this simple change in position, the metrestick will support a lot more weight. That is because the stiffness of a beam is in proportion to its height. A beam on its edge is higher than a beam laid flat, and so is stiffer. Next time you see a house or a deck being constructed, look at how the supporting beams are placed under the floor or ceiling.

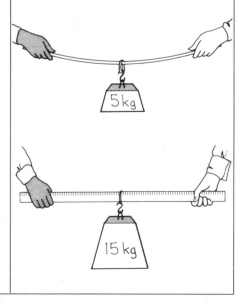

Why do your ears pop when you ride in an airplane or a tall elevator

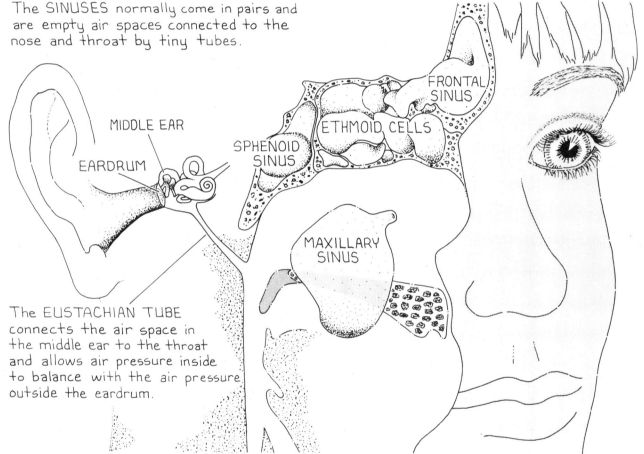

The SINUSES normally come in pairs and are empty air spaces connected to the nose and throat by tiny tubes.

MIDDLE EAR

EARDRUM

SPHENOID SINUS

ETHMOID CELLS

FRONTAL SINUS

MAXILLARY SINUS

The EUSTACHIAN TUBE connects the air space in the middle ear to the throat and allows air pressure inside to balance with the air pressure outside the eardrum.

Your ears pop whenever you change altitude because of the changing air pressure. We live, in fact, at the bottom of an ocean of air. Right at the bottom – at sea level – the air feels heaviest. The higher up you go the less weight the air has, and the less pressure there is on your body.

When you ride up in an elevator or an airplane, you are moving rapidly into an area of lower air pressure. As a result, the small air spaces at the back of your nose and inside your ears expand. The air escapes through tiny tubes in your head and you hear a popping noise.

When you come back down again, the outside air pressure increases, and those air spaces in your head are squeezed. You feel pressure on your ears, and sometimes you hear squeaky noises as the air squeezes back into your head through tiny tubes. You can help relieve the pressure by pinching your nose, then by gently trying to blow through it. This balances the air pressure between the inside and the outside of your ears.

A. Collapsing Can

Things you need
- empty pop can
- pair of tongs
- large bowl of cold water

What to do
1. Pour just enough water into the can to cover the bottom.
2. Place the can on a stove and heat it until the water boils and you see steam coming out of the opening.
3. When the water has boiled for about thirty seconds, carefully grasp the can with the tongs.

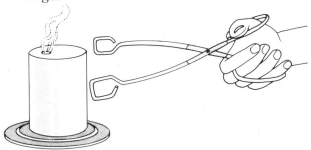

4. As quickly as possible, turn the can upside down in the bowl of water, making sure that the open end remains below the surface of the water.
5. Watch what happens to the can.

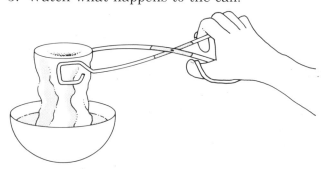

Explanation

When the can full of steam was turned upside down in the bowl of cold water, the steam rapidly cooled. As it did this, it condensed back into water, reducing the pressure inside the can. The pressure of the air on the outside of the can was greater, and caused the can to collapse. At the moment of collapse, the air exerted a force of about 266 kg (580 lb) on the outside of the can.

B. Make a Bottle That Breathes!

Your lungs are not muscles. They operate by air pressure applied from the outside. Here's how you can make a working model of your lungs.

Things you need
- large plastic pop bottle
- 2 plastic straws (The bendable kind are best.)
- 2 balloons
- 2 elastic bands
- modelling clay or tissue paper

What to do
1. Tie the two balloons on the ends of the straws using the elastic bands. Make sure the balloons will still inflate when you blow through the straws.

2. Push the straws into the neck of the plastic bottle so the balloons are hanging down inside.

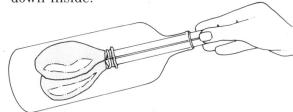

3. Seal the neck of the bottle around the straws with modelling clay or a wad of tissue paper.

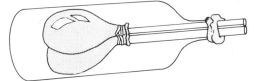

4. Squeeze and release the sides of the bottle and watch what happens to the balloons.

Explanation

Your lungs work in the same way. They inflate and deflate because of the pressure exerted when your chest expands and contracts. Feel your ribs while taking deep breaths, and you will feel them moving in and out.

■ The weight of the air resting on your head and shoulders is more than 450 kg (992 lb). You don't collapse like the can because most of your body is made of liquid, which does not compress, and the air pockets inside your body are at the same pressure as the pressure of the atmosphere.

■ When whales and dolphins dive deep in the ocean, the pressure of the water causes their lungs to collapse. This does not hurt the animals because they do not use their lungs underwater. Sea mammals can remain submerged for many minutes because they store extra oxygen in their blood.

■ Scuba divers have to pop their ears constantly as they dive deeper to balance the pressure of the air cavities in their heads against the pressure of the water. Water pressure is so great that even a change of a few metres in depth will affect the ears.

■ When a tornado passes over a house, the extremely low pressure in the centre of the funnel causes the air inside the house to expand. The expansion is so fast that the house explodes.

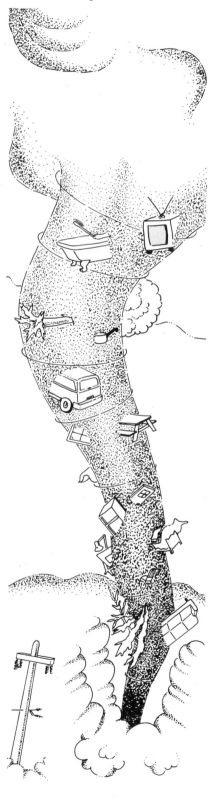

■ Jet fighter pilots, who change altitude quickly, cannot carry ballpoint pens in their pockets. If there are any air bubbles in the pen, they will expand when the plane climbs, bursting the pen and spewing ink all over the pilot's uniform.

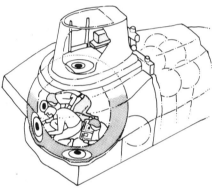

■ Submarines that are able to reach the bottom of the ocean are made of superstrong titanium metal. They are shaped like a ball so they can stand pressure from all sides at once. Their strength makes sure they will not collapse under the many tonnes of water pressure.

■ Airliner cabins have to be pressurized so the people will be comfortable when the plane is flying at extremely high altitudes. Otherwise, the passengers' ears would pop so much it would be extremely painful. The air pressure inside the plane also makes sure that there is enough oxygen for everyone to breathe.

What makes a ball bounce

Balls bounce because they are made of elastic materials like rubber or soft plastic. Elastic materials bend out of shape when a force is put on them, then return to their original shape when the force is released. This ability to spring back into shape is called **elastic energy.**

When a ball falls to the floor, it has energy because it is moving. When it hits the floor, the force of the collision flattens the ball slightly and makes a small dent in the floor. When the floor and the ball spring back to their original shapes, their elastic energy is turned into motion. Since the floor cannot move very far, most of the energy goes into the ball, which bounces back into the air. Balls with more elastic energy, the springier ones, bounce farthest, while soft sponge balls do not bounce as high. If the floor has no elastic energy, the ball will not bounce at all. Try dropping a ball onto sand. It does not bounce because the sand has very little elastic energy and absorbs all the motion.

KITCHEN DEMO

Bounce or No Bounce?

Things you need
- several balls of different types
- ruler

What to do
1. Stand the ruler on end, and hold a ball at the 30 cm (1 ft) mark, measured from the bottom of the ball.
2. Drop the ball from this height onto a table and try to catch the ball on its first bounce.
3. Measure how high the ball bounced. You may have to try this several times to make sure you catch the ball at the highest point in its bounce.
4. Repeat the experiment for each ball. Why do you think the balls bounce to different heights? What would happen if the wrong ball was used for a sport like baseball?

5. Place a smaller ball on top of a larger one.
6. Carefully drop both balls together from 30 cm and watch what happens.
7. Experiment by placing different balls on top of each other and dropping them together.

Explanation

The height to which the balls bounce depends on how much elastic energy they have. Balls that don't bounce very high turn the energy of their collision with the table surface into heat rather than motion.

Normally a ball will not bounce higher than the original height it was dropped from. An exception is when a lighter ball is placed on top of a heavier one and then dropped. When the two balls hit the floor together, the lighter one takes off and bounces higher than the 30 cm it was dropped from. This is because the large ball transfers its energy of motion to the smaller one. This gives the smaller ball more energy than it would normally have on its own, so it flies much higher. The larger ball, meanwhile, has lost all its energy to the smaller one, so it does not bounce at all. This is how you can take the bounce out of a superball: Just place a squash ball on top of it!

47

DID YOU KNOW ???

■ Shock absorbers on a car absorb the elastic energy of the rubber tires. Without shocks the wheels would bounce like balls every time the car hit a bump!

■ A billiard player relies on the elastic energy of the billiard balls and the sides of the table to bounce the balls off each other and win the game.

■ When astronaut George Nelson tried to hook onto the Solar Max satellite floating freely in space, his hooking device did not work. When he bumped into the satellite, the elastic energy of the collision sent both of them spinning.

■ The front and rear sections of cars are designed to crumple in a crash so they will absorb the elastic energy of a collision. If they did not do that, the cars would bounce off each other like rubber balls, then continue to bounce off other objects until they came to a stop.

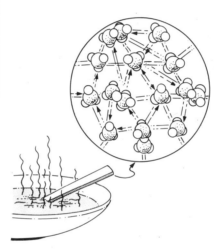

■ When one end of a metal spoon is left in hot soup, the molecules in the metal gain energy and begin to bounce off each other. This bouncing causes other nearby molecules to move and the bouncing motion produces heat. The motion of the molecules gradually works its way up the handle. If the spoon is left in the soup long enough, all those bouncing molecules in the handle will make it feel hot when you try to pick the spoon up.

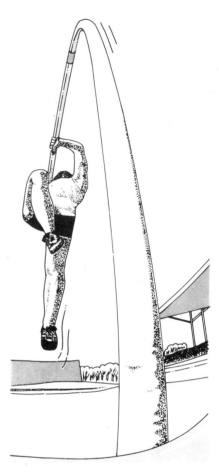

■ The large air bags used by pole vaulters and high jumpers have very little elastic energy. The bags absorb the energy of the athletes as they fall to the ground so their bodies will not bounce into the air again.

■ Official balls used in professional sports are tested to make sure they have the right amount of bounce. Can you imagine what would happen if a superball was used in a baseball game? Every hit would be a home run!

Why does the sound of a siren change when a fire truck passes by ?

Sirens, horns, and even the noise of a passing car, all seem to change from a high sound to a lower one as they pass a person standing still.

Sound is produced by waves that travel through the air. When the sound waves are produced by a moving object, the waves spread out in all directions. The waves travelling forward, in the same direction as the fire truck are bunched together and shortened by the motion of the vehicle. This bunching of the waves in front of the truck causes the sound of the siren to rise as it approaches a person standing on the sidewalk. The waves that go out the back of the truck are stretched out by the motion, so the sound of the siren gets lower as the truck passes. The driver of the fire truck does not hear the sound change at all because the distance of the driver from the siren remains the same.

This effect was first measured by Christian Doppler in 1842. He asked several musicians to play one continuous note on their trumpets while riding on a train. Doppler stood beside the tracks and listened to their sound as the train passed. From this experiment, he was able to measure how much the sound waves changed when the train was approaching and when it was leaving. He also noticed that the effect was greater as the speed of the train increased. He then placed the musicians beside the tracks and rode the train himself, and he heard the same effect. The change in waves caused by motion is now called the Doppler effect.

The Swinging Alarm Clock

Things you need
- mechanical alarm clock with a bell, or digital watch with an alarm
- piece of *strong* string 2 m (6 ft) long
- friend

What to do
1. Tie the string firmly to the alarm clock.
2. Wind the clock up fully and set the alarm.
3. Adjust the time until the alarm goes off.
4. When the alarm starts ringing, begin swinging the clock in a circle over your head while your friend stands a safe distance away.
5. Gradually let the string out to its full length and listen to the sound of the alarm.
6. Change positions with your friend and repeat the experiment with your friend swinging the alarm clock. How is the sound of the clock different when you hear it from a distance compared with the way it sounded when you were standing in the centre of the swing circle?

Explanation
The alarm produces sound waves of one frequency. When you are swinging the clock, the distance between the alarm and your ear does not change once the string has been let out, so you hear no Doppler effect when you swing the clock. To persons standing farther away, the distance between their ear and the alarm is always changing. The clock is approaching them on one side of the swing, and moving away on the other half of the swing. These persons will hear the sound of the alarm rising and falling because of the motion. The Doppler effect can be increased by making the string longer and swinging the clock faster.

■ The Doppler effect works for all kinds of waves, including water waves, light waves, radar waves, and radio waves.

■ Astronomers measure the Doppler shift of light waves from distant stars to tell whether the stars are moving towards the Earth or away from it. Those moving towards us have light that looks blue, while those moving away look red.

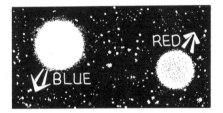

■ Some stars show both a blue and a red shift in their light. Astronomers think that is because the gravitational pull of their planets causes the stars to wobble back and forth, just like the swinging alarm clock. By measuring the Doppler shift in the light, astronomers have calculated that these unseen planets are bigger than Jupiter.

■ Bats use the Doppler effect to "see" in the dark. They make high-pitched clicks that bounce off objects. The time it takes the sound to return to the bat's ears measures the distance to the object. If the object is moving, such as a flying insect, the Doppler effect will change the frequency of the reflected sound. The bat then knows which way and how fast the insect is moving.

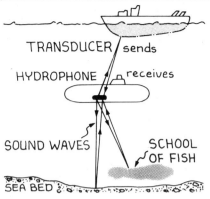

TRANSDUCER sends
HYDROPHONE receives
SOUND WAVES
SCHOOL OF FISH
SEA BED

■ Submarines don't have windows, so they use sonar to see underwater. Sonar uses sound waves that are bounced off the sea bottom to measure depth. These sound waves reflect as well off other ships, so the submarine can determine the direction, speed, and location of nearby ships.

■ Whales and dolphins use echolocation to see underwater and communicate with each other. Sound waves travel four times faster underwater than in air.

■ Doctors use the Doppler effect to create pictures of unborn babies. The technique, called **ultrasound**, sends sound waves through the mother's body. The sound waves change their speed, depending on whether they are passing through skin or bone. This changes their frequency. The device turns the frequency changes into a "sound picture." This method is safer than X-rays because there is no radiation used, just ultra-high-frequency sound.

■ Police use the Doppler effect to catch speeders. A radar device sends out a radar beam, which bounces off the speeding car. The device measures the reflected waves and senses the change in frequency caused by the motion of the car. That is automatically translated into a speed, which sometimes translates into a ticket for the driver.

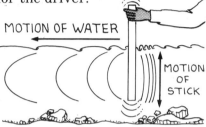

MOTION OF WATER
MOTION OF STICK

■ If the end of a stick is vibrated up and down in a stream of water, the waves on the upstream side of the stick will be shorter than the waves on the downstream side because of the motion of the water.

Try this
Jingle bells

ting
BR-RING

Using two bicycles that have bells, you and a friend ride toward each other while you both ring your bells. (WARNING: Be careful not to have a collision!) Compare what happens to the sound of the bell on your bike with the sound coming from the other bike at the moment you pass each other. Try it at different speeds and see if the effect changes.

How can you tell if an egg is raw or boiled without cracking it

You can tell if an egg is raw just by giving it a spin. A boiled egg will spin easily, and when you stop it, it will stay stopped. A raw egg will resist spinning at first. Then, once you get it spinning and stop it, the egg will start up again on its own!

This is because of **fluid resistance**. When you first try to spin the raw egg, the liquid inside remains still for a short while, slowing the egg down. If you keep trying, the liquid will begin to spin with the egg. When you suddenly stop it, and then let go, the liquid keeps spinning for a while, which starts the egg moving again.

Fluid resistance is caused by the friction between a liquid and the sides of the container that holds it.

Racing Soup Cans

Things you need

- several unopened cans of soup, each a different kind (Make sure all the cans are the same size and weight.)
- two bottles or jars with lids, both the same size and shape
- water
- a board at least 1 m (3 ft) long

What to do

1. Place some books under one end of the board to make a ramp. The ramp does not have to be steep.
2. Place two of the soup cans side by side at the top of the ramp, let go of them at the same time and see which one gets to the bottom first.
3. Race all the cans against each other until you have an overall winner and loser. What is the difference between the soup that won and the soup that lost?
4. Roll the two empty bottles down the ramp. They should tie.
5. Half fill one bottle with water and race the bottles again. Try the race with one bottle completely full and the other one half full. Do you think the weight of the water has anything to do with which bottle wins?

Explanation

The cans roll at different speeds because the thickness of the fluid inside each is different. Mushroom soup, for example, is very thick. It has a lot of resistance and does not roll well. Onion soup is runnier and spins up more quickly. This allows the can to roll faster.

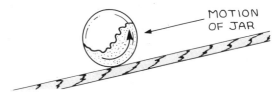

When the bottle was half filled with water, it rolled more slowly because the water piled up on the back side of the glass. This puts more weight on the back side, and that slows the bottle down. When the bottle is completely full, it rolls faster because the water is evenly distributed, so there is no pile-up. The weight of the water has little to do with it, although the bottle that is full will roll farther than an empty one.

53

■ High-speed liquids and gases, such as steam, build up a lot of resistance in the pipes when they are forced to go around corners. So high-speed pipelines are made as straight as possible, with only very gentle curves.

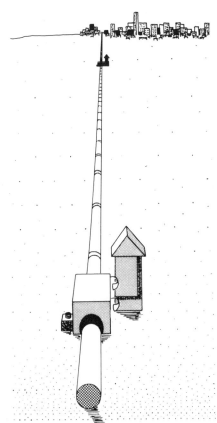

■ Oil and gas pipelines that cross the country need pumping stations at intervals along the lines to keep the fluids moving. Otherwise, the resistance between the fluids and the sides of the pipe would cause the liquids to slow down and eventually stop. A single pump on one end of the pipe would not be strong enough to push even gases through.

■ Tanker trucks have baffles – plates with small holes in them – inside the tanks. This prevents the liquid from sloshing around. If the baffles weren't there, the liquid would pile up on one side of the tank when the truck went around a corner, causing it to tip over.

Does light always travel in straight lines

No. Light can be bent around corners using fibre optics. Fibre optics are made of very long, thin pieces of glass, about the thickness of human hair. These glass fibres can bend without breaking. When light is shone down one end of the fibre, the inside of the fibre acts like a mirror, bouncing the light back and forth, keeping it trapped inside the fibre. The only place the light can get out is at the other end. Even if the fibre is bent, or tied in a knot, the light still makes it all the way through.

If thousands of fibres are packed into a cable, each one can carry a different beam of light. By pulsing the light beams on and off very quickly, messages can be sent and received using the light beams instead of electric currents.

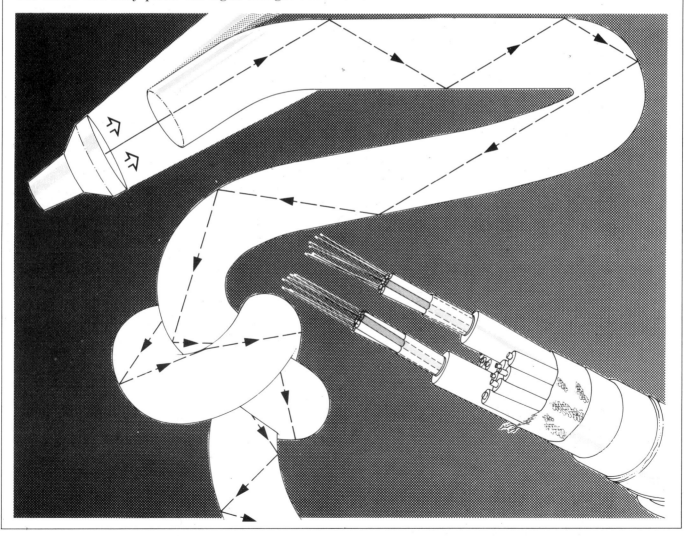

KITCHEN DEMO

Pouring Light

Things you need
- flashlight
- piece of black paper
- glass jar with a metal lid
- large bowl
- black tape
- hammer
- nail
- water

What to do

1. Using the hammer and nail, punch a hole in the lid of the jar 2 cm (3/4 in) from the rim.
2. Punch another hole on the opposite side, 2 cm from the rim. Make the second hole bigger than the first.

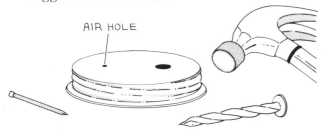

AIR HOLE

3. Lay the jar on its side and place the flashlight against the bottom.

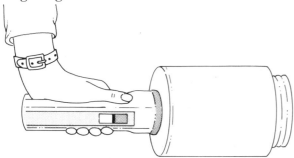

4. Wrap the black paper around the flashlight and jar, making a light-tight seal.

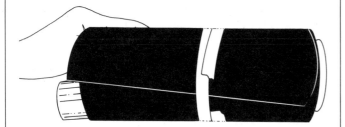

5. Wrap more tape around the top of the jar, covering the glass just up to the threads at the rim.

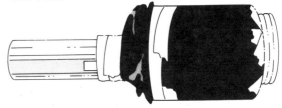

6. Remove the flashlight and fill the jar three-quarters full of water.
7. Put the lid on tightly.
8. Turn on the flashlight and insert it back into the the paper tube against the bottom of the jar.

9. Darken the room, then pour the water out of the large hole into a bowl. Why does the inside of the bowl light up?

Explanation

The inside surface of the water stream acts like a mirror. This keeps the light rays inside the stream so it follows the curve of the falling water. When the light shines out the end of the stream, it is pointing down into the bowl, causing the inside of the bowl to shine.

DID YOU KNOW ???

■ Polar bear fur is not white. Each hair is a clear, hollow tube that acts like a fibre optic thread. The hairs guide sunlight down to the bear's black skin, where it is absorbed and helps keep the bear warm. (A solar bear!) All the hairs together reflect and scatter light, making the fur appear white. Snow crystals, which are also not white, do the same thing.

■ A device called a light pipe uses long plastic prisms to guide sunlight into buildings. Light pipes look like ordinary lights, except they brighten and dim when clouds pass over.

■ The first communication using a beam of light was sent by Alexander Graham Bell in 1880. He called his invention the photophone.

■ Thousands of optical fibres can be bundled together into a fibre optic cable. In theory, all the telephone calls in the world could be carried at the same time in one fibre optic cable.

■ In hospitals, laser operations can be performed from outside the body by inserting two tiny fibre optic cables into the patient. One carries a laser beam, the other allows the doctor to see inside the body during the laser surgery.

What's so special about the North Star

If a top is spinning at an angle, it will move slowly in a tilted circular motion. This movement is caused by gravity trying to pull the top down while the top is trying to remain upright. The tilted circular motion is called **precession.**

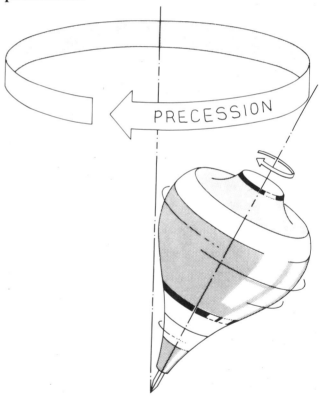

The Earth is like a giant gyroscope. It keeps spinning with its axis pointed in one direction.

The North Star, named Polaris, just happens to be located almost directly over the Earth's north pole. The spinning of the Earth keeps the pole pointing at that star, so it is the only star in the sky that appears to be standing still. (There is no star over the south pole.)

The Earth does the same thing as the gravity of the Sun and Moon try to pull it over. In the future, the north pole will swing away from Polaris and point to another star called Vega. But don't worry about losing our North Star tomorrow, or even during your lifetime. The precession of the Earth is extremely slow. It takes about 26 000 years for one wobble to happen. People will not be using Vega as the North Star for another 12 000 years.

KITCHEN DEMO

Gyroscopically Stabilized Lifting Body

Things you need
- two styrofoam coffee cups
- sticky tape
- 12 elastic bands

What to do

1. Tape the bottoms of the cups together so they form a kind of cylinder with the open ends facing outward.

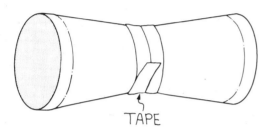

TAPE

2. Tie the elastic bands end to end to make a chain.

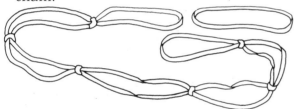

3. Hold one end of the elastic chain against the tape in the centre of the cups, then wind the elastic chain loosely around the cups until there is about 15 cm (6 in) left.

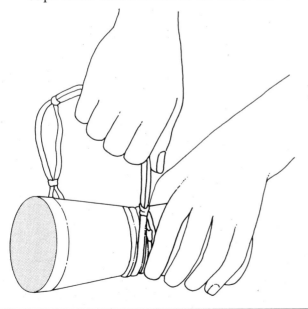

4. Hold the cups by the centre so the elastic comes out of the bottom. (You want the cups to spin backwards.)

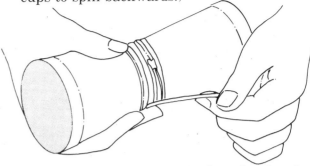

5. Stretch the loose part with the other hand and launch the cups straight ahead of you. It may take a few tries. How far can you make the cups fly?

Explanation
The spin of the cups turns them into a gyroscope, which keeps them pointed in the same direction as they travel through the air. Because the cups are spinning backwards, air moves over the top of the cups faster than the air that moves under them. This causes low pressure above the cups and high pressure below. The pressure difference produces lift, which is what holds the cups in the air.

DID YOU KNOW ???

■ When archaeologists study ancient ruins that were built to record the positions of the stars, they have to remember that the stars were in different positions in ancient skies because of the wobble of the Earth.

■ A frisbee can be called "a gyroscopically stabilized low angle of attack lifting body," but it's easier to call it a frisbee!

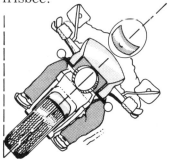

■ The wheels of a motorcycle are gyroscopes, so when the driver puts pressure on one of the handlebars, the wheels begin to precess, causing the bike to lean as it goes around a corner.

■ Large telescopes have to cancel out the motion of the Earth in order to track the movements of stars across the sky. Part of the computer program that steers the telescope computes the slow wobble of the Earth's axis.

■ Gyroscopes are easy to make. Try making different types using the items in the drawing.

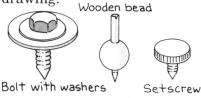

Wooden bead

Bolt with washers   Setscrew

■ Ships and aircraft that travel across the north pole must rely on gyroscopic compasses because magnetic compasses point south when you are at the north pole!

■ Uranus is a planet that spins sideways as it goes around the Sun. No one knows why, but one theory is that planets occasionally topple over, just like tops that develop wobbles and then start spinning sideways. Perhaps Uranus is halfway through a topple.

60

Why do you get thrown to the side when a car goes around a corner

When any object is in motion, it wants to keep moving at the same speed in the same direction. That's one of the laws of motion discovered by Sir Isaac Newton. This tendency to not want to change is called **inertia**. When the car you are driving in goes around a corner, inertia tries to keep your body moving in a straight line. As a result, you get pushed to the outside of the turn. For the same reason, you also get pushed forward when the car stops because your body wants to keep going.

Once the car is stopped, and you are still again, the law of inertia says you want to stay that way. So when the car starts up once more, you are pushed into the back of the seat! In other words, inertia wants to keep an object doing whatever it's doing – to resist any change.

KITCHEN DEMO

The Backward Ball

Things you need
- table tennis ball
- string
- sticky tape
- tall glass jar
- water
- scissors

What to do
1. Using the tape, attach one end of the string to the table tennis ball. (Wrap it around more than once to make sure it stays on.)

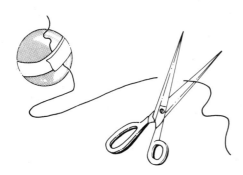

2. Cut the string so it is the same length as the height of your jar.
3. Tape the loose end of the string to the inside bottom of the jar. Make sure the ball does not stick above the rim of the jar when the string is straight.

4. Hold the jar upside down and move it quickly back and forth. Watch the motion of the ball compared with the jar.

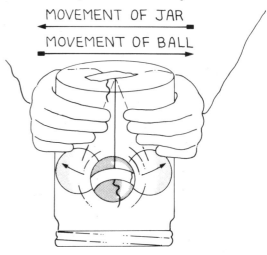

MOVEMENT OF JAR

MOVEMENT OF BALL

5. Fill the jar with water until it completely covers the ball. Hold the jar in your hand, and quickly move it in different directions. How has the motion of the ball changed compared with the motion of the jar?

MOVEMENT OF JAR

MOVEMENT OF BALL

Explanation
When the jar is empty, the inertia of the ball makes it behave like your body in a moving car. It lags behind when the motion starts, and keeps moving when the jar stops. When the jar is full of water, the inertia of the water makes it slosh to the back when the jar starts moving. This makes the water pressure higher on the back side of the jar. The ball, being lighter than water, moves to the area of low pressure, which is forward, in the same direction as the movement of the jar. The opposite happens when the jar stops. The water sloshes forward, and the ball is pushed to the back, exactly opposite to what your body does in a moving car.

■ Once a spacecraft climbs above the Earth's atmosphere and reaches its orbital speed of 40 000 km/h (24 800 mph) the engines are shut off and its inertia keeps the spacecraft going around the Earth for weeks or even years.

■ In a car accident, people are injured most when their inertia keeps their bodies moving after the car has stopped. The victims actually crash into their own cars!

■ Magicians use inertia to pull the tablecloth out from under dishes. If the tablecloth does not drape over the edge of the table, it can be snapped out quickly enough that the inertia of the dishes will keep them in place. (If you try this yourself, start with plastic dishes!)

PREPARE TO BE AMAZED!

■ The reason you don't fall out of your seat on a looping roller coaster is because your body wants to keep moving in a straight line while the coaster curves up and over. Your inertia is strong enough to keep you in the seat even when you are upside down. Of course, inertia also lifts you out of your seat when the coaster goes over the top of a hill.

■ A helium balloon suspended in the middle of a car will move opposite to what your body does when the car starts, turns, or stops. The balloon is pushed by the air in the car, which sloshes around like the water around the table tennis ball in the Kitchen Demo.

■ Astronauts on the Moon found it tricky to walk. Because of the Moon's lower gravity, they did not weigh as much, but they still had the same amount of inertia. This meant that, once they started moving, they had to skid to a stop as though they were on ice.

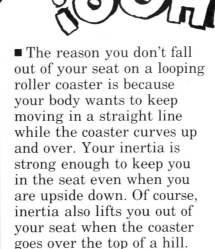

¡YA-HOO!

Try this
Bottle Challenge

Place a dollar bill on top of a bottle, then balance another bottle the same size on top of it. Challenge a friend to remove the bill without toppling the top bottle. If the friend just pulls, the bottle will fall. The secret is to hold the loose end of the bill firmly, then with your other hand, do a karate chop, snapping the bill downward. Be careful not to hit the table or the bottle with your chop. If you are fast enough, the inertia of the top bottle will hold it in place while the bill snaps out from under it.

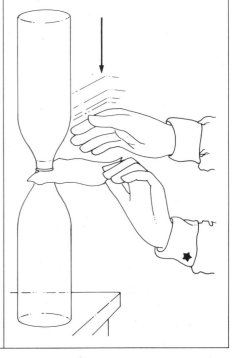

Why do knuckles pop

Knuckles and knee joints have fluids in them that act like oil to make the joints work smoothly, so that you won't squeak when you walk. The liquids also contain gases. When a knuckle is stretched, the pressure on the fluid is lowered. This allows the gases to expand, and they pop out to form bubbles. That is the popping sound you hear. Once knuckles have been popped, it takes about fifteen minutes for the bubbles to be re-absorbed back into the liquid. That's why knuckles can't be popped twice in a row.

KITCHEN DEMO

Eyedropper Diver

Things you need
- large plastic pop bottle with cap
- glass eyedropper
- tall glass
- water

What to do
1. Fill the tall glass with water.
2. Half fill the eyedropper with water.
3. Turn the eyedropper upside down and tap the sides so that the little air bubble escapes.
4. Squeeze the bulb again and add more water to the dropper.
5. Try floating the dropper in the glass of water. If it sinks, squeeze out a little bit of the water until the dropper just barely floats.

6. Fill the plastic bottle almost to the top with water.
7. Carefully lift the eyedropper out of the glass and drop it into the plastic bottle.

8. Put the cap tightly on the bottle, then squeeze the sides tightly. Watch the eyedropper. See if you can suspend the dropper in the middle of the bottle.

Explanation
When you squeeze the plastic bottle, you are applying pressure to the water. Water does not compress, but air does. So the water squeezes the little air space inside the eyedropper.

As the air space gets smaller, more water enters, making the eyedropper heavier and causing it to sink. When the pressure is released, the air space expands, pushing the water out. The dropper then floats. When the dropper neither floats nor sinks, it is at neutral buoyancy. This is what fish and submarines do to remain suspended in the water.

■ When scuba divers spend a long time at great depth underwater, they have to come up slowly. Otherwise, gas that has been forced into their blood by the water pressure will pop out, forming bubbles. Divers call this the "bends." The bends are extremely painful and can even cause death.

■ Submarines change the amount of air in their ballast tanks to make the sub rise or sink. When just enough air is in the tanks, the sub will remain at neutral buoyancy. If the sub dives, the air in the tanks will compress and shrink. Extra air has to be pumped in to allow the sub to level off, otherwise it would keep on sinking.

■ Some people suffer aches in their joints when bad weather comes along. The lower air pressure of a storm causes the gases in their joint fluids to pop out, causing the pain. ("I'm one of those people who can predict the weather by the way my knees feel." – Bob McDonald)

■ Soda pop has gas dissolved in the liquid just like the liquids in your knuckles. When you open a bottle, the gases are released and you see bubbles rising. This is the same process as the release of gases in your knuckles when they crack.

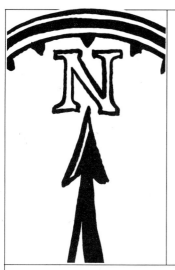

Does a compass always point north

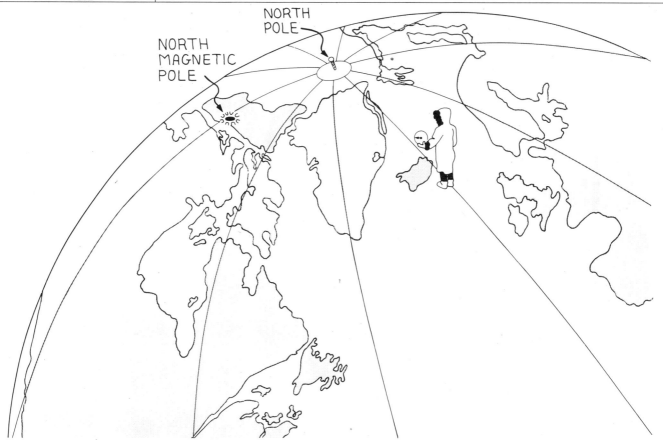

NORTH POLE

NORTH MAGNETIC POLE

No, it doesn't! If you are at the north pole, a compass will point south! The Earth has two north poles. One of them is true north, the point at one end of the Earth's axis. The other is the magnetic north, which is about 1400 km (870 miles) away from true north.

A compass needle is a small magnet balanced on a pin so that it is free to point in any direction. Since magnets are attracted to each other, the compass needle lines itself up with the magnetic north.

No one knows exactly how the Earth generates its magnetism, but it is believed to come from the molten iron in the Earth's core. All magnets have fields, or areas where their pull can be felt. The Earth's magnetic field is so large that we are always in it, which is why a compass always points north.

Many metals, such as iron, that remain in a magnetic field for a long time will become magnets themselves, so many magnets can be found naturally. It was the discovery of a magnetic rock, first known as **lodestone**, in the 1100s that enabled ships to sail out of sight of land and still know where they were. The lodestone always pointed north.

Paper Clip Balloon

Things you need
- paper clip
- small magnet
- glass jar with a metal lid
- piece of thread

What to do

1. Stick the magnet to the underside of the lid of the jar. The magnet should stay there on its own.

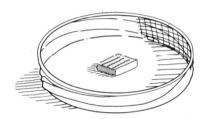

2. Tie one end of the thread to the paper clip.
3. Tape the other end of the thread to the bottom of the jar. The paper clip should almost reach the lid of the jar when the thread is straight.

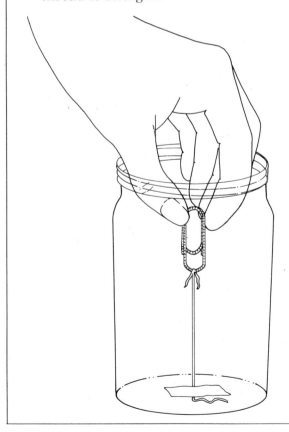

4. Put the lid on the jar and turn it upside down so the paper clip hangs down near the lid.
5. Turn the jar over, and the paper clip should remain suspended in the centre of the jar without touching anything.

6. Try shortening the string to see how far you can get the paper clip to levitate. Once you get it as low as possible, tell your friends you have a paper clip balloon inside the jar!

Explanation

The paper clip is attracted to the magnet. The field of the magnet extends one or two centimetres away from its surface. The lowest position in which the paper clip levitates is where the force of the magnetic field is the same strength as the force of gravity on the paper clip.

■ The north and south magnetic poles of the Earth have reversed positions at least a dozen times in the past.

■ Migratory birds such as geese, can detect the magnetic field of the Earth. It is believed that they use this to find their way south every winter, then return to the same nesting grounds every summer.

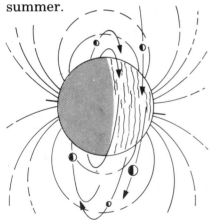

■ The planet Uranus has a magnetic field that is sideways to the north and south of the planet. The centre of the magnetic field is not located at the centre of the planet as it is on Earth. It is believed that Uranus has this unusual magnetic field because much of the planet is made of hot water, which conducts electricity. The water can easily move around, carrying the magnetic field of the planet with it.

■ Your bathtub may be a giant magnet. If the bathtub in your home faces north or south, hold a compass at one end of the tub and watch the needle. Do the same thing at the other end of the tub. If the compass needle reverses, the tub has been magnetized by the magnetic field of the Earth.

Try holding the compass at the top and bottom of the tub. There may be another north pole and south pole there, because in Canada, the magnetic field lines of the Earth run at a downward angle to the ground.

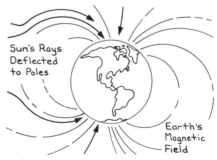

Sun's Rays Deflected to Poles

Earth's Magnetic Field

■ The magnetic field of the Earth steers particles from the Sun toward the north and south poles. When these particles enter the Earth's atmosphere, they glow, producing the northern lights (aurora borealis) and southern lights (aurora australis) in the sky.

■ You can make a compass from a coat hanger. Unwind the hanger into a straight wire. Tie a piece of thread to the centre of the wire so that the wire balances when you suspend it from the thread. Hang the wire in the middle of a room, then close all the doors and windows in the room. Do not disturb the wire for at least a day. Then slowly open the door, taking care not to create a draft, and look at the wire. It should be pointing north-south because it has been magnetized by the Earth.

How do polarized sunglasses work ?

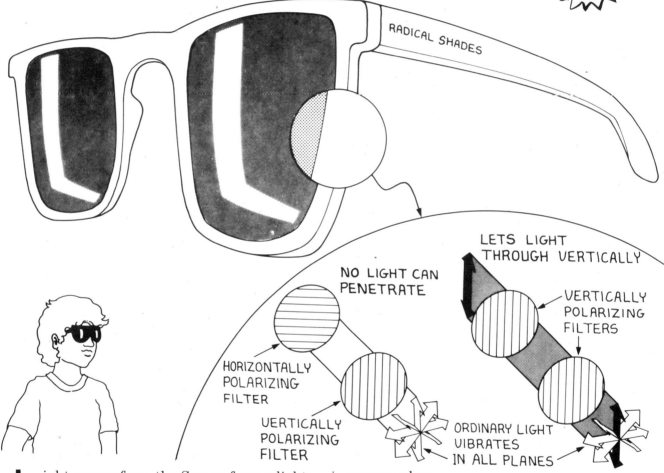

RADICAL SHADES

NO LIGHT CAN PENETRATE

LETS LIGHT THROUGH VERTICALLY

VERTICALLY POLARIZING FILTERS

HORIZONTALLY POLARIZING FILTER

VERTICALLY POLARIZING FILTER

ORDINARY LIGHT VIBRATES IN ALL PLANES

Light waves from the Sun or from a light bulb vibrate in all different directions. Polarized filters, like the ones in sunglasses, only allow light waves vibrating in one direction to pass through. If you could make yourself very tiny and look at the glasses, you would see long molecules lined up like the sticks of a picket fence. The light waves that are vibrating in just the right direction will pass through the narrow slits between the molecules. All other light waves will be blocked. This is how the sunglasses remove glare.

Polarized filters can also be used to stop light completely. If two filters, one that stops waves vibrating sideways and one that stops waves vibrating up and down, are placed together, the light that makes it through the first filter will be blocked by the second. That's how you can tell if glasses are polarized. When two pairs are placed together, and one of them is rotated, the glasses should completely block out all light and appear black.

A Colourful World

Things you need
- an old pair of polarized sunglasses
- clear cellophane tape (not the frosted kind)
- plastic wrap
- anything made of clear plastic (for example, a picnic fork, toothbrush, or glass)

What to do
1. Put the sunglasses on and look around while tilting your head from side to side. Try looking at a shiny tabletop, the sky, or the surface of a puddle.

2. Carefully take one of the glasses apart and remove the lenses.
3. Hold one lens in front of the other and look out a window or at a bright light. Rotate one of the lenses.

4. Have a friend hold the two lenses while you stretch a piece of cellophane tape between them. Do the same thing with a piece of plastic wrap. Stretch it, roll it into a ball, and unfold it, all the while looking through the two filters.

5. Hold a clear plastic object between the filters and bend it in different directions. (Be careful not to break it!)

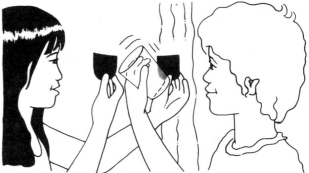

Explanation
Many sources of light around you are polarized. For example, the sky, and the light reflecting off a shiny table. When you tilt your head while wearing the glasses, you are filtering out some of this light. This makes the sky darker, and the glare comes and goes on the surface of the table. Plastics are made of long molecules that also polarize light. When the plastic is stretched or bent, the molecules become twisted. This actually twists some of the light passing through it, separating the colours. Some colours are twisted more than others. The polarized lenses stop some of the colours and let others through. The colours that make it through are the ones you see.

DID YOU KNOW ???

MR. ANT

DIRECTIONS 5¢

■ Ants and honeybees can detect polarized light from the sky. They use the polarization as a direction finder so they can make their way back to the nest or hive.

I SEE SPOTS BEFORE MY EYES.

BUT I CLEANED THE WINDSHIELD.

■ When wearing polarized glasses, you can sometimes see blue spots on car windows. These are stress marks where the layers of glass have been pressed together. It's the same effect as stretching the plastic wrap in the Kitchen Demo.

■ Electronic watches that have LCD (liquid crystal displays) use polarization to make the numbers. The glass covering the watch is one polarized filter and the liquid inside contains free-floating polarized crystals. Electric patterns are set up that cause some of the crystals to rotate so that they block light and form the shape of the numbers.

■ Polarized filters for cameras can be used to remove some of the light coming from the sky. This makes the sky look darker blue to the camera, producing a more dramatic picture.

■ When light shines on a smooth surface like water, the light waves that reflect off the surface are all vibrating in the same direction. These light rays are polarized. If polarized filters are lined up so only light waves vibrating up and down will get through, the sideways-vibrating waves that have bounced off the water will be blocked, making fish visible.

■ When scientists first saw rocks brought back from the Moon, the rocks seemed dull and grey. When the rocks were sliced into very thin sections and examined through polarized filters, many colours appeared. They were produced by minerals within the rocks, some of which had never been seen before.

■ Plastic models of bridges or buildings are sometimes studied through polarized filters. Putting weights on the models makes colourful patterns where the structure bends. Knowing where the stresses are, the structure can be redesigned or made stronger in those places.

Colourful patterns show stress

5 kg   2 kg   2 kg   5 kg

How does a record make sound

Records are plastic discs that are covered with tiny grooves. If you look at the surface of a record with a magnifying glass, you will see that the grooves look like wiggly lines. Actually, there is only one groove that runs from the outside of the disc and winds many times around, ending up at the centre. When the sharp needle of the turntable is placed on the spinning record, it follows this groove. The wiggles in the groove cause the needle to vibrate back and forth. The vibrations are turned into electrical impulses. These are amplified, then turned into sound by the speakers.

The more wiggles there are, the faster the needle vibrates, and the higher the sound. Low sounds don't have as many wiggles. Look closely on the record and see if you can spot different sizes of wiggles. The wiggles show up better on the single-song 45 records.

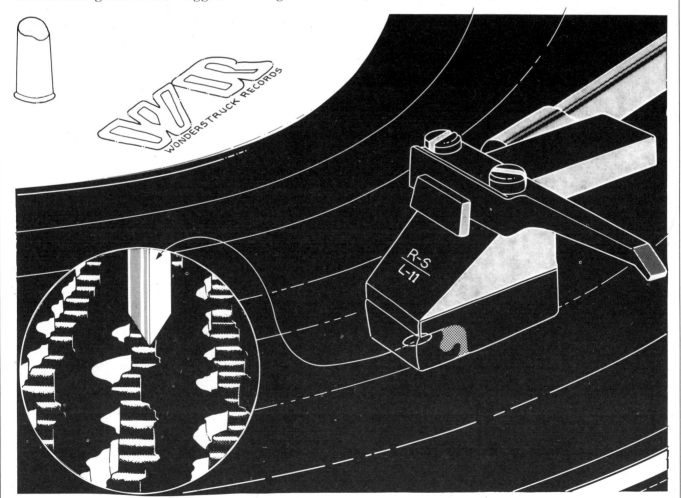

KITCHEN DEMO

A Paper Player

Things you need
- an *old* 45 record, or your own 45 record (After this demo, the record cannot be played on a normal record player again, so make sure you get permission to destroy this one.)
- piece of stiff paper
- pin or needle
- tape
- record turntable

What to do
1. Form the piece of paper into a cone, and use the tape to fasten the edges.
2. Tape the needle to the small end of the cone so that 1 cm (1/2 in) of the needle sticks out beyond the end of the paper.
3. Place the record on a turntable and set it spinning at 45 r/min.
4. Carefully lay the needle in the groove on the outside of the disc and let it follow on its own. Do not hold the cone tightly, and do not try to guide the needle, or it will skip. Listen to the sounds produced by the cone.

Explanation
The grooves of the record cause the needle to vibrate. The vibrations of the needle are transferred to the cone of paper. Because the cone is larger than the needle, it moves more air as it vibrates, producing a louder sound. Playing the record at different speeds changes the speed of the vibrations, so the sound is lower when the record is slow and higher when the record is fast.

DID YOU KNOW ???

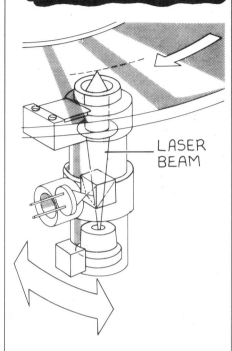

LASER
BEAM

■ Compact discs use laser beams instead of needles to play the music. Tiny pits in the disc cause the beam to vibrate back and forth. A light detector senses the flickering beam and translates it into music. The advantage is that the disc does not wear out because the only thing that touches it is light.

■ Jet engines whistle with a high-pitched sound because their blades spin at very high speeds – about 20 000 revolutions per minute.

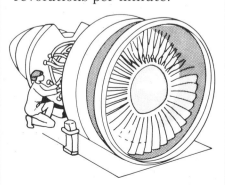

■ An electronic device enables some sound recordings to be sped up without causing a change in pitch. The voices sound normal, but very fast. The device is sometimes used in fast-talking television commercials to cram more than a minute's worth of talk into a one-minute commercial.

It slices dices cubes purees liquifies and generally mushes things up try the latest thingama-jig guaranteed to satisfy or your money cheerfully refunded but act today at this price these handy gadgets won't last!

WOW!

■ A balloon can be made to sing. Inflate the balloon, then pinch the end with your fingers as you let the air out. If you stretch the end while pinching it, the pitch of the sound will change, giving you higher and lower notes.

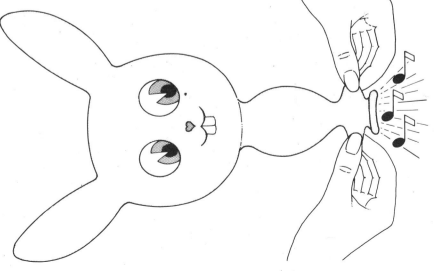

Why do some words appear backward in a mirror ?

Look at this picture in a mirror!

Mirrors are a reflection of the world, not a true picture of it. Everything in a mirror appears backward because light waves reflect straight off the surface. When you read a word on a piece of paper, the page is facing you. To look at it in a mirror, you have to turn it around, away from your face, to see it in the mirror. The words are now backward to your eyes. It's this reversed image that you are seeing reflected in the mirror.

Some letters of the alphabet, like the letter A, do not turn backward because they are symmetrical. If you divide the letters down the middle, they look the same on one side as they do on the other. Symmetrical letters do not turn around in a mirror.

KITCHEN DEMO

Fun with Mirrors

Things you need
- 3 pocket mirrors (You can get them in a drugstore.)
- some pieces of paper thin enough to see through when you write on them
- tape

What to do
1. Stand behind a friend and look at each other in one of the mirrors. How do you look different to each other?
2. On the piece of paper, print out all the letters of the alphabet. Make sure you can see the letters through the back of the paper. (If they are dim, trace over them on the back of the paper.)
3. Hold the front of the paper up to the mirror and look at the image of the letters. Which letters did not turn around? How are these letters different from the ones that did turn backward? How does the image in the mirror compare with the letters as they appear through the back of the paper?

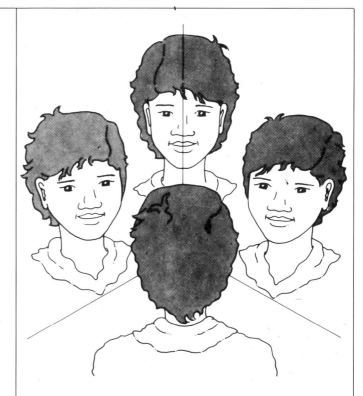

4. Turn the paper around and look at the image of the letters on the back side.
5. Try to make words that will look the same in the mirror as they do on paper.

6. Using tape, attach two mirrors by their edges so they make a 90° corner. Look at your alphabet in this arrangement. Look at your face in the two mirrors. This is the way the rest of the world sees you. Try combing your hair while looking into these mirrors.

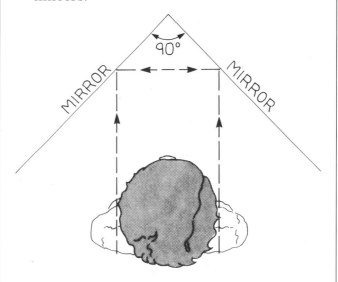

Explanation
The angle of the two mirrors causes light rays to bounce off one mirror, then cross over to the second mirror before returning to your eyes. When the image bounces off the second mirror, it reverses again, which means it goes back to the way it was. It's the only time a mirror reflects the real world.

Hockey Rink Optics

You can make a model of light rays hitting a mirror.

Things you need
- a friend
- 2 hockey sticks
- 2 tennis balls or rubber balls
- hockey rink with boards

What to do
1. Stand several metres away from the boards with your friend beside you. At the same time, shoot both balls straight at the boards. The balls should come straight back.
2. Have your friend move a little farther down along the boards. Bounce the balls off the boards so they return to your friend. Compare the angle that the balls hit the boards with the angle that they leave.
3. Move to the corner of the rink and repeat the straight in shot. Make sure that the balls hit slightly off the centre of the corner. With practice, you should be able to get the ball to cross over to your friend, and your friend to get a ball to come to you.

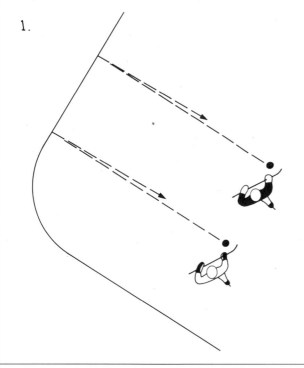

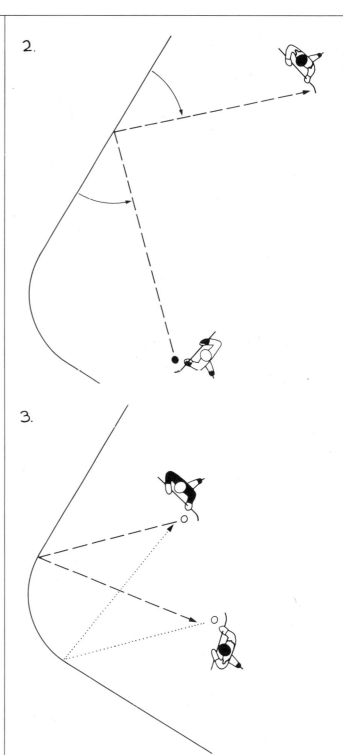

Explanation
The balls represent light rays, which always travel in straight lines. The boards are like a mirror. When flat, the light rays reflect off at the same angle they come in.

The corner of the rink represents a curved, or concave, mirror. The crossing of the balls is what happens when the light rays hit a curved mirror, producing an upside-down image. You can see this effect by looking at your face on the inside of a spoon.

DID YOU KNOW ???

THAT'S BETTER.

■ Some large telescopes use mirrors, which means that astronomers are often looking at an upside-down image of the Moon!

■ Many people think they look terrible in pictures. A picture shows how you look the right way around, not the backward way you appear in a mirror.

■ A dentist uses a mirror to see the teeth at the back of your mouth. Special training is needed to learn how to work while looking at an image that is backward.

■ The world's largest telescope will have a mirror made of many sections. Each piece will be controlled by a computer to make it shimmer, which will take the twinkle out of the starlight in the mirror.

■ In cameras, or other systems that use mirrors, a second mirror is sometimes added so that the image will not be backward.

■ When scuba divers look up at the surface of the water from below, they sometimes see a mirror image of the bottom. This is similar to the way you see the mirror image of clouds when you look at the surface of the water from above.

 Try this

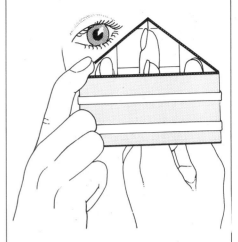

Tape three mirrors together to form a triangle with the shiny sides facing in. Hold your finger in the centre of the triangle, and see how many images you can get at one time. Carefully hold the triangle up to your eye and look through it at objects in the room. This arrangement of mirrors is called a **kaleidoscope.**

Find pictures in a magazine that show faces looking straight at you. Hold a mirror on its edge so that it divides the face right down the centre of the nose. Look at the complete face that forms in the mirror. Now turn the mirror around, and compare the image you get looking at the other side of the face. Are they any different?

What is a mirage?

A **mirage** is an image of a distant object produced when light is bent by the Earth's atmosphere. The bending of light is called **refraction**, and it happens whenever light passes from one medium to another. The light could be passing from air into water, or into glass, or even from cold air into warmer air.

A mirage appears on days when the sky is clear and there is no wind. As the Sun heats the ground, a bubble of warmer air rises up, under the colder air above. Although you can't see it, the edge of the bubble is curved, like a giant lens. Light passing through this boundary will be bent, so a person looking along the horizon can actually see over the curve of the Earth to distant mountains. The more the light is bent, the higher into the sky the mountains seem to float. In the desert, light can be refracted upwards, so an image of the sky appears in the sand, looking much like a lake. The effect only works during certain conditions and at certain angles. So a mirage will disappear by the end of the day.

KITCHEN DEMO

A. Sunset Mirage

Things you need
- large plastic pop bottle
- pile of books
- piece of paper
- marker pen

What to do
1. Fill the plastic bottle with water all the way to the top.
2. Making sure that there is no air bubble inside, put the cap on the bottle and tighten.
3. Lay the bottle on its side, and make a pile of books almost as high as the bottle. You should just be able to see about one-quarter of the bottle when you look along the top of the books.
4. On the piece of paper, make a large dot that is just below the height of the books when the paper is stood on end.
5. Hold the paper with the dot behind the bottle and look along the top of the books. You should be able to see the dot through the bottle.

6. Without moving the paper, remove the bottle and look along the books again. The dot should disappear.
7. Empty the bottle, and try the experiment again without the water. Can you see the dot when there is only air in the bottle?

Explanation
The water in the bottle refracts the light rays that have bounced off the dot. The rays were bent to your eye so you could see the dot in the same way distant mountains are seen in a mirage. The effect doesn't work with air in the bottle, because air is less dense than water and doesn't refract light as much.

B. Wow Your Mom!

1. Print the word WOW on a piece of paper.
2. Using the plastic bottle filled with water, hold it sideways several centimetres above the paper and look through the bottle at the words.
3. Then print the words CARBON DIOXIDE on another piece of paper and repeat step 2. Why do some words turn upside down and others don't? Can you make words that do not turn upside down when seen through the bottle?

Explanation
The water in the torpedo bottle is acting like a lens. Light rays passing through the water cross, producing an upside-down image. Some letters of the alphabet, like X, have top halves that are the same as the bottom halves, so the letters look the same upside down. Try looking at the word MOM in a mirror. How does it look upside down?

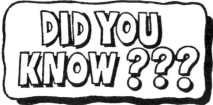

DID YOU KNOW ???

■ It is believed that mirages helped Erik the Red travel from Iceland to Greenland. Islands over the horizon sometimes become visible as mirages. This could have helped Erik "island hop" across the Atlantic Ocean.

■ Mirages don't just happen in hot deserts. They are frequently seen in the Arctic. The frozen, dry North is also classified as a desert; it's just a cold one.

■ Highway signs look bright in car headlights because the signs are coated with paint containing glass beads. Light from a car's headlights is turned around by the beads and bounced back to the driver.

■ Millions of tiny glass beads are in the soil on the surface of the Moon. When sunlight strikes the beads, the light is bounced back like a highway sign, making the Moon brighter than it would be if it was covered with ordinary dirt.

Why do you hear the sound of the sea in a sea shell

What you are really hearing when you put a sea shell to your ear are the sounds around you being amplified by the air space inside the shell. The effect is called **resonance**, and it happens whenever waves fit exactly into a container and amplify themselves. Sound waves are vibrations in the air. When these waves enter the space inside the shell, they bounce around and become louder. The size of the shell determines the sound you get. A large shell will produce low sounds with longer sound waves. A small shell will produce higher sounds. Resonance is used a great deal in musical instruments, such as guitars, where the air space in the body of the guitar amplifies the sound of the vibrating strings.

Canned Sound

Things you need
- several containers of different sizes (tin cans, glass jars, long tubes)
- 2 bottles of the same size and shape

What to do
1. Hold each container to your ear and listen to the different sounds they produce. Can you identify the sounds in the room that are being amplified by each container?
2. Repeat the experiment in different rooms and outside.
3. Blow into one of the bottles until you produce a note. Bring the second bottle to your ear while still blowing into the first.

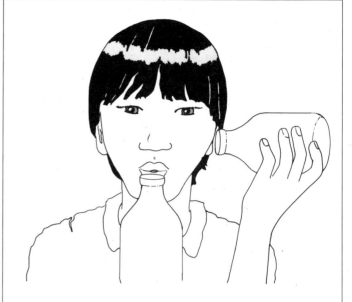

4. Stop blowing and listen closely to the second bottle.
5. Give one bottle to a friend and have the friend make a note while you listen to the other bottle. Then you blow and have the friend listen.

Explanation
Each container resonates with different sounds in the room, amplifying those frequencies, just like a sea shell. The strangest sound comes from a long tube because its air space is quite large.

When a musical note is produced by blowing on the bottle, those sound waves resonate and are amplified in the space of the second bottle. This happens because those sound waves fit exactly into that space. When a complete wave will fit inside a container, that container will resonate.

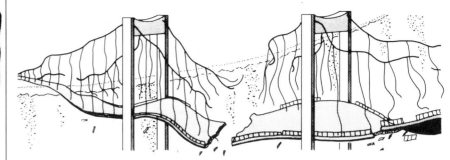

DID YOU KNOW ???

■ You can play a guitar or piano without touching it. Open the cover of a piano and hold down the loud pedal (the one on the right) and shout into the strings. You will hear your voice in the strings because those strings that are the right length will resonate with the sound vibrations of your voice. Try making high sounds and low sounds, and listen to which strings in the piano resonate. The same thing can be done by singing different notes into the hole of a guitar and listening to the strings.

■ The exhaust pipes of race cars are just the right length to resonate with the sound of the engine. The resonance makes it easier for the exhaust gases to flow through the pipe, and it also makes the engine sound louder, which some people prefer.

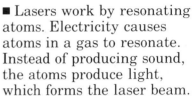

■ In 1940 a large suspension bridge across the Tacoma Narrows in the state of Washington began to resonate with the wind. The deck of the bridge began to twist back and forth with such violence that the bridge completely tore itself apart in about an hour.

■ Anything will vibrate, even tall buildings. On certain days, some buildings will resonate with the wind and begin to sway back and forth. In some cases this swaying has been enough to make people on the top floors seasick.

■ A microwave oven uses resonance to cook. Microwaves are a form of radiation that resonates with water molecules. The molecules begin to vibrate when exposed to the microwaves, causing them to get hot. It's the heat of the water that cooks the food.

■ Lasers work by resonating atoms. Electricity causes atoms in a gas to resonate. Instead of producing sound, the atoms produce light, which forms the laser beam.

■ Some water pipes are shaped in such a way that air bubbles form in the water. The bubbles begin to vibrate and the pipes resonate. This causes the "hammering" heard in some walls when the water is turned on at a certain speed.

Why do wagon wheels seem to turn backward in western movies ?

Backward-turning wagon wheels in movies are caused by the **stroboscopic effect**. Movies are made of many still pictures that flash on and off twenty-four times every second. Your eye cannot see the flashes, so your brain fuses all the pictures together into one smooth motion. If a wagon wheel is turning at just the right speed, the spokes will be in one position for one picture. During the twenty-fourth of a second before the next picture, the wheel rotates so that the next spoke is now in the position the first one was in. When the second picture is taken, a spoke will still be seen in the same position, even though it is a different spoke. At this speed, the wheel will not seem to be turning at all. If the wheel turns a little faster than the speed of the film, the spokes will seem to move slowly forward. If the wheel turns a little slower than the film, the spokes will appear to turn backward. That is because the second spoke did not quite make it up to the position of the first spoke by the time the second picture was taken. The following spoke will be a little later and so on. This apparent backwards motion is called **migration**. It happens when a rotating object is looked at under a flashing light.

KITCHEN DEMO

Build a Stroboscope

Things you need
- piece of cardboard
- scissors
- push pin or thumb tack
- cork

What to do
1. Cut the cardboard into the two shapes shown in the illustration. Make sure the hole is as close to the centre of the circle as possible.
2. Cut out the slot in the handle
3. Cut out only one of the slots in the wheel.
4. Push the pin through the hole in the wheel, then through the hole in the handle. Push the cork onto the pin so it holds the two pieces loosely together. The wheel should be able to turn freely.
5. Hold the slit in the handle up to your eye and look through it while spinning the wheel.
6. Look at a television screen, at the blades of a turning fan, or at the spokes of a spinning bicycle wheel. What happens when you cut more slots in the wheel?

Explanation
When the slot in the wheel lines up with the slot in the handle, you are able to see through for a brief period. The speed of the wheel and the number of slots determine the frequency with which you see. A television picture flickers on and off thirty times a second. The black bars you see across the picture are part of the scanning process that makes up a television picture. Your stroboscope can appear to stop the blades of the fan or the spokes of a bicycle wheel for the same reason wagon wheels appear to go backward in a movie. The stroboscope is acting like the shutter in a movie camera.

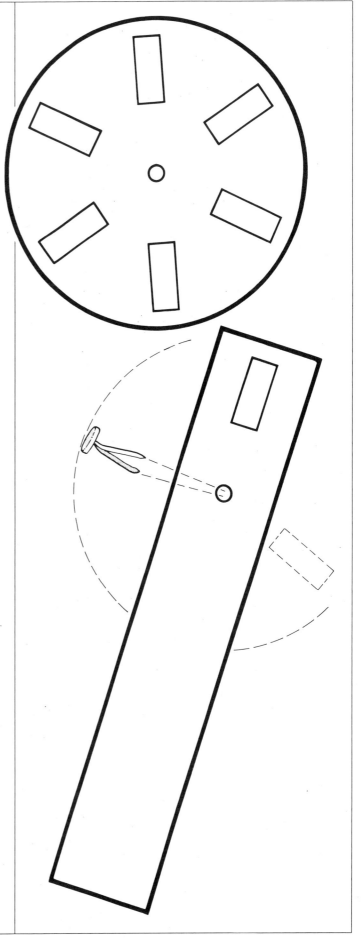

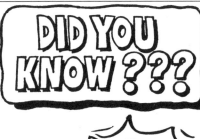

DID YOU KNOW ???

■ Stroboscopes were used with cameras in 1850 for high-speed photography. Using very strong lights and very powerful flashes, photographers could freeze the action of a bullet coming out of a gun barrel.

Try this

Hold your hand in front of a television screen and quickly wave your hand back and forth. The stroboscopic effect of the flickering screen will make it appear that you have six fingers and three thumbs.

■ Fluorescent lights (the long white tubes) flash on and off sixty times a second. The human eye cannot detect the flashes, but a fly, with its more sensitive eyes, can see every flicker. To a fly crossing a room, the lights are going completely off and on again. What appears to be an ordinary room to us must appear like a disco to a fly!

■ If you hum to yourself while watching television, you can sometimes see bars across the screen. If you raise or lower your hum, you can make the bars rise and fall. Your humming is vibrating your head in synchronization with the flickering television screen.

Why do figure skaters speed up when they pull in their arms during a spin

Anything that spins turns about an axis, like a wheel around its axle. An object with a shape that is spread out away from the axis, takes more energy to spin than an object with a shape that is closer to the axis. If a skater starts spinning with the arms extended, a certain amount of energy has been used. That energy is contained in the spinning motion. When the arms are brought in close to the body, the body changes to a slim shape that does not need as much energy to spin that fast. The extra energy has to go somewhere, so the speed of the spin increases. If the skater wants to slow down, the skater simply extends the arms once again.

High divers do the same thing when they want to control their spin while in the air. They tuck in tightly to spin faster and then stretch out to slow down for a smooth entry into the water. When scientists want to know how much energy it will take to spin something, they not only have to know how heavy that object is, but also what shape it has.

Roller Races

Things you need
- several solid balls, such as baseballs or rubber balls (not hollow ones)
- several objects shaped like discs, such as a flying disc, a pie plate, or a hubcap
- several objects shaped like rings, such as an old tire or a hula hoop
- a long board for a ramp or a gentle, smooth hill

What to do
1. Choose one of each type of object and have a race down the ramp or hill. Race all the objects against each other in this way. What type of object always wins?
2. Line up the objects in order, starting with the winner and ending with the loser. Look at the shape of each object. Which object has the most spread-out shape?

Explanation
The balls always win because they have their mass closer to their axis and, therefore, it takes less energy to spin them. A ring takes the most energy to spin because its mass is farthest away from its axis.

■ Cars with smaller engines have smaller wheels, so the engine does not have to waste as much energy getting the wheels to spin.

■ Large spinning wheels hold so much energy when they spin, they have been used to power buses in Europe. The wheel slows down as it loses energy to move the bus, but then the bus gives some energy back to the wheel, spinning it faster again as the bus comes to a stop.

■ A hurricane is a spinning storm. As it gets stronger, the spiral shape gets smaller. This causes the storm to spin faster, creating extremely high winds on the ground. It's the winds that do much of the damage to buildings.

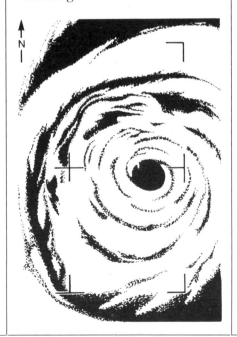

■ When some satellites are launched into orbit, they are set spinning. When the antennae of the satellite are extended, the spin slows down. Engineers who launch the satellite have to know how much it will slow down, so there will still be enough spin left to keep the satellite stable.

Why do objects sometimes appear upside down in a magnifying glass

A magnifying glass is a lens, which is a piece of glass or plastic that bends light through **refraction**. A lens has a different thickness in the centre than at the edges. If you lay a magnifying lens flat on a piece of newspaper, there will be very little difference between what you see through the lens and what you see with your eye. As you lift the glass off the newspaper, the words will become larger, or magnified. If you keep raising the glass, you will reach a point where the image in the glass becomes blurred and then flips upside down. The distance between the lens and the paper when the image flips over is called the **focal length** of the lens. Once you pass the focal length, the light rays have completely crossed and the image will remain down.

A Can Camera

Things you need

- 500 ml (16 fl oz) plastic container with a misty "see through" lid (If the lid of the container isn't transparent plastic, you can use a piece of wax paper instead.)
- magnifying glass (glass or plastic)
- black paint (optional)
- knife

What to do

1. Cut a round hole in the bottom of the plastic container that is slightly smaller than the lens of the magnifying glass.

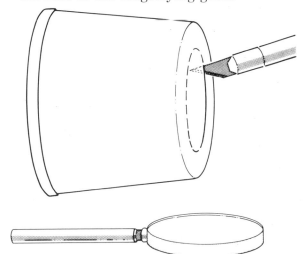

2. Paint the inside of the container black.

3. Put the lid on the container or cover the top with a smooth piece of wax paper.
4. Hold the container up to a window with the lid facing toward you and the magnifying glass covering the hole.
5. Adjust the distance between the magnifying glass and the hole until you get a clear image on the lid.

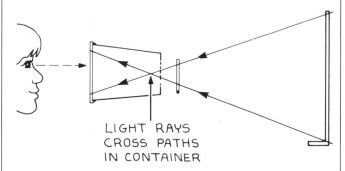

LIGHT RAYS CROSS PATHS IN CONTAINER

Explanation

Light rays coming through the magnifying glass lens are focused on the lid of the plastic container, producing a clear image of the scene outside the window. The image is upside down because the rays cross in the middle of the plastic container. The distance between the lens and the lid has to be adjusted to make images of objects close up or objects far away.

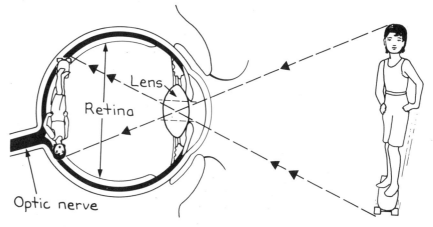

Lens

Retina

Optic nerve

■ A camera lens produces an upside-down image on the film just like the one on the lid of the plastic container. Chemicals in the film react to light, producing a photograph.

■ The word lens is Latin for "lentil bean." In the fourteenth century, early eyeglass lenses were thick and fat, reminding their makers of lentils. It's a good thing they didn't call them beans!

■ You cannot see well underwater because your eyes are designed for seeing in air. Some fish have bifocal lenses in their eyes. The top half of the lens is for seeing in air, the bottom half is for seeing underwater.

■ Soft contact lenses float across the surface of the eye on a river of tears. They allow water to pass through so the eye does not dry out.

■ Contact lenses and glasses distort incoming light to cancel out the distortions caused by imperfect lenses in the eyes. The clear vision that results shows that sometimes two wrongs make a right.

■ The small lenses in your eyes produce upside-down images of the world on the back of your eyeballs. Your brain turns the images right side up so you don't get confused.

■ In 1608, a Dutch eyeglass-maker named Hans Lippershey held two lenses up to the window and looked through them both. He saw an upside-down magnified image of a distant church steeple and accidentally discovered the telescope.

■ Camera lenses are made of several pieces because the different colours in sunlight bend different amounts. With only one lens, some of the colours would be out of focus. The extra pieces cancel out this effect and assemble all the colours together onto the film.

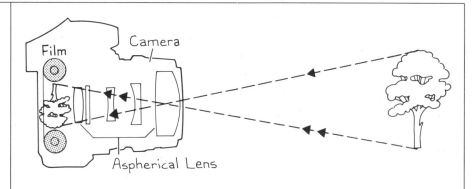

Film
Camera
Aspherical Lens

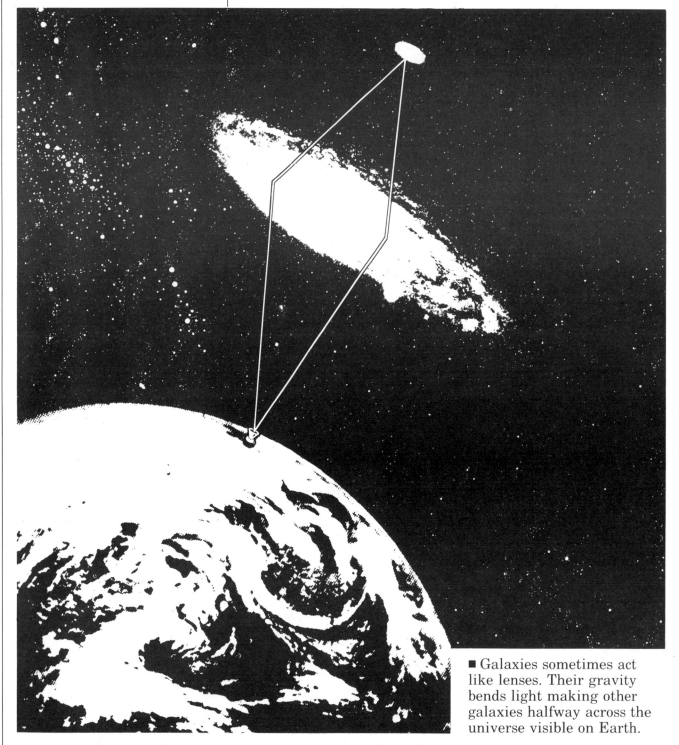

■ Galaxies sometimes act like lenses. Their gravity bends light making other galaxies halfway across the universe visible on Earth.

Do scientists have all the answers ?

No, and that's what makes science so interesting. Very often a scientific experiment raises more questions than answers. There are still many more good questions that have no answers. For example:

1. What colour were the dinosaurs?
2. What causes ice ages?
3. Is there life in space?
4. Where did the Moon come from?
5. How do caterpillars turn into butterflies?
6. Why do some people get sick in space and others don't?
7. Can people make machines that "think"?
8. What do singing whales say to each other?

Index